BRIDGE TO NOWHERE

Larry R. Humes

It was the kind of story reporter Brad Norris had always hoped for. Rare treasures salvaged from a Spanish galleon suddenly disappeared, and the girl who had taken them killed herself. When the police couldn't find either the body or the goods, Brad decided to do a little investigating of his own, and what he came up with was murder!

BRIDGE TO NOWHERE

Larry R. Humes

Curley Publishing, Inc.
South Yarmouth, Ma.

Library of Congress Cataloging-in-Publication Data

Humes, Larry R.
  Bridge to nowhere / Larry R. Humes.
     p. cm.
   1. Large type books. I. Title.
  [PS3558.U4443B7 1990]
  813'.54—dc20
  ISBN 0–7927–0298–0 (lg. print)   89–23810
  ISBN 0–7927–0299–9 (pbk.: lg. print)   CIP

Published in Large Print by arrangement with Dorchester
Publishing, Inc. in the United States, Canada, the U.K. and
British Commonwealth.

Distributed in Great Britain, Ireland and the
Commonwealth by CHIVERS LIBRARY SERVICES
LIMITED, Bath BA1 3HB, England.

Printed in Great Britain

BRIDGE TO NOWHERE

1

Sunday night for a police reporter is normally a quiet affair. Liquor stores are closed and most lawbreakers are out of money as the weekend draws to a close.

However, there are exceptions. Like the night the museum call came over the radio.

It was shortly after 11 P.M. and the city edition had just gone downstairs to composing. I was sitting at the city desk glancing over the page proofs when the three high-pitched tones came over the police scanner.

"All units in the vicinity of 1600 Carondolet Lane – a signal 32 in progress. Silent – approach with caution," said the woman's voice through the nearby speaker on the wall.

A routine burglar alarm call in a city the size of Jacksonville is no big deal. However, the address on Carondolet sounded strangely familiar.

"That address ring any bells?" I asked Hank Nichols, the night city editor who was sitting nearby.

"Nope," he replied, looking up from his

proofs. "Why don't you check the cross-reference directory?"

A quick check confirmed my suspicions – the address on Carondolet was the address of the Jacksonville Museum of Modern Art.

"Of course," I blurted out. "The museum. We ran a story the day before yesterday on the recovered treasure they have on display over there." Grabbing a notepad and pencil, I bolted through the newsroom and headed for the parking lot.

"I don't wanna be here all night," Nichols hollered behind me. "If it looks like anything, give me a call and we'll replate."

"Right, I'll call on the radio," I replied, not bothering to wait for the elevator but heading for the stairs at the rear of the building.

The city of Jacksonville is divided by the St. Johns River which meanders through its center. The museum is located on the southside – about fifteen minutes from the office. Crossing the Main Street Bridge at a fast clip, I monitored police units on the scanner as they closed in on the block-long, two-story building.

"Unit 4320, am approaching the building now," a voice crackled out of the speaker mounted under the dash. "There doesn't appear to be any sign of activity." The policeman's transmission was followed by

2

several other officers talking back and forth amid the static.

"Hey, you guys," added one patrolman, "as I was coming down the street, I noticed a late model Grand Prix, maroon with a black vinyl top, heading in the opposite direction. Any of you see it?"

"Was a young woman driving it?" asked another voice.

"Yeah," replied the officer. "You got her in sight?"

"No, but she passed me just a second ago. I'll go back and check it out."

I pulled up in front of the museum as one officer crawled through a broken glass panel of the front door and another stood behind him, shotgun poised. A patrolman I had run into before stood in the street near his patrol car.

"Hey, Bendix, what's going on?" I asked.

"You know as much as me," he said in a gruff, nervous manner. "I suggest you stay out of sight, though, until we're sure no one is in there."

I stepped into the street, placing the police car between myself and the museum. I might be relatively new at reporting but I'm not stupid.

The officer who had disappeared inside the museum suddenly reappeared and waved to the others in the street that the burglars had made good their escape.

"What did they steal?" I yelled before he slipped inside again.

"Can't tell yet," he hollered back and then was gone.

I remembered from the article we had run two days before that the treasure was valued at about $1.5 million. It had been discovered, the story stated, somewhere off the Florida Keys in the wreckage of a two-hundred-year-old Spanish galleon.

My thoughts were suddenly interrupted by the patrolman's call for help coming from the speaker of the squad car parked in front of us.

"Stand by for a signal 35," said the voice of the woman dispatcher. Her voice was followed by that of the patrolman who had been chasing the woman in the red Pontiac.

"Unit 4350 requesting back-up," said the voice with an inflection suggesting urgency. "I've got a woman driving a 1975 Pontiac, eastbound in the 1500 block of State Street. She's headed for the Andover Bridge and she's ignoring my lights and siren."

Before the dispatcher could comment, the voice of another officer came across the channel.

"This is 4315," said the voice. "We're ahead of you in the eastbound lane of the bridge right now. We'll set up a roadblock about one hundred fifty feet west of the toll booth. All you have to do is drive her into us."

Racing toward the bridge, I called Nichols on the radio and requested "photo" send a man to meet me there.

"Oh my God! She jumped off the bridge!" the officer screamed into his keyed mike. "I don't see her. Better call Marine Patrol and see if they can get out here on the double."

Burying the accelerator in the floorboards, I nearly drove into a parked car. It was probably too late for tomorrow's edition, I figured. Perhaps enough time to replate a bulletin of about five column inches or so. Enough to show the publisher we were at least awake. But this was the kind of news a reporter waits for – the kind of story that will make him known. I wasn't about to call it a day at that point.

"Roger 4350. What's your 10-20?" asked the dispatcher.

"I'm right in the middle of the bridge," the patrolman answered. "She jumped from the middle of the bridge. While you're at it, you'd better call homicide 'cause this has got to be a seven."

It was a clear summer night and the lights of the bridge reflected in the distance like a

5

string of pearls against a black velvet cloth. I could make out the flashing blue lights halfway across as I approached the bridge on State Street. At the scene, traffic was backed up. Leaving the car, I ran ahead to find a crowd beginning to gather at the railing. The bridge was four-laned so the westbound lane continued to move, although the rubber-neckers kept it slowed to a snail's pace.

The policeman's car was stopped in the middle of the eastbound lane, the maroon Pontiac in front of it. The patrolman was searching through the back seat of the woman's car with a flashlight while a growing crowd of onlookers watched with blank expressions on their faces.

"Hi, officer, I'm Brad Norris of the Jacksonville *Chronicle*," I said, waving my press card in his direction. "How come she jumped?"

"Beats me. I was a good two hundred yards behind her when she just slammed on the brakes, jumped out of the car, and leaped over the railing there. It wasn't like anyone was chasing her or anything. And she sure didn't fall over that railing by accident. From what I could see, it looked like she was in a hurry to kill herself." As he talked,

6

he continued to search under the car seats for any identification or sign of the stolen treasure. Meanwhile, the patrolmen who had set up the roadblock at the foot of the bridge came running up and began helping to get the traffic moving again.

"You found anything yet she could have taken out of the museum?" I asked.

"Nope," he replied. "If she took anything, she either threw it out the window or had it on her when she jumped, 'cause this car is definitely clean."

The patrolman went back to his cruiser to run a computer check on the license plates while I walked over to the railing. It looked to be about a one hundred fifty-foot drop to the water below. A freighter had just passed beneath on its way out to sea, churning up the river and sending ripples splashing against the grassy banks. I could also make out the silhouette of a small marine patrol boat below as it scanned the black water with its search-lights, hoping to find some evidence of the unidentified woman's body.

"Hello, Brad." I turned to find Cris Carroll, a reporter with WFLA-TV, standing behind me. She was unraveling the cord to her micro-phone while the cameraman with her stood nearby focusing the lens of his mini-cam. In addition to her stunning beauty, Cris was a good reporter, one of the best in local television.

"Know what happened?" she asked.

"Not yet, Cris. Just got here myself."

"Any sign of the leaper down there?"

"Doesn't look like it," I replied. I leaned against the railing and watched as Cris did a short interview with the cop. She stayed just long enough to get his narrative of what happened and then began packing the gear in order to get back to the studio and make the 11 o'clock news. I always enjoy watching the television people work. Writing for newspapers is a hell of a lot easier since all you need is a pencil and paper. But the TV people are like a traveling roadshow. They can't move without drawing a crowd of gapers who insist on standing in the background and waving at the camera. And where many people don't mind being quoted in the paper, they either refuse to stand in front of a television camera or freeze up completely. I wouldn't want to do it. But it is a delight to stand by and watch what they have to go through. Makes my job seem easier.

"Going to be in the office later, Brad?" Cris asked as she lugged her equipment toward their van.

"For a little while," I replied. "Give me a call if you need a hand."

With the help of a few bystanders, the cop managed to push the Pontiac against the railing so traffic could begin moving again. As motors cranked and traffic began to creep by the abandoned automobile, I noticed Wink McCormick approaching with his camera strapped over his shoulder.

"Am I too late for the party?"

"Yeah, it looks like it," I replied.

Wink was a burly black man with bushy eyebrows and a neatly trimmed pencil mustache. In his late forties, he was a real professional. Wink had been around newspapers for at least thirty years and was the best photographer at the *Chronicle*, hands down. Nobody knew his first name – they all called him Wink because he could be depended on to be at the scene of a disaster in the wink of an eye. A reporter in the Deep South often faces the possibility of getting pushed off a story by the typical redneck sheriff. And if you're black, that's two strikes against you. Jacksonville had changed a lot during the 60s but everyone still looked up to Wink for having been a first-rate reporter when being black wasn't so fashionable.

After snapping a picture or two of the car as a city wrecker backed up in preparation for hauling it away, Wink exchanged a few words with the young patrolman filling out the report and then made his way over to the railing. I called a couple of graphs into Nichols on the radio and then joined McCormick at the side of the bridge.

"Anybody see her jump?"

"Apparently not, Wink," I replied. "The cop chasing her said she just skidded to a stop and jumped over the railing here. These scratches in the paint are fresh. Probably made by her belt buckle or something."

"Yeah, probably," Wink said. "Soon as he finishes his report, maybe we can get a shot of him pointing to the scratches and then get out of here."

"I guess so. Don't imagine they'll figure this thing out tonight, anyway."

"Have they found the body yet?"

"Not yet," I replied. "I've been keeping an eye on that marine patrol boat down there and they still have their draglines out. The thing that puzzles me is why she would want to jump from the middle of the bridge anyway. Even if she saw the roadblock down there near the toll booths, she must have realized she didn't stand a chance of making it from up here. Why commit suicide over a lousy handful of jewels?"

Wink snapped the lens cover on his camera and dropped it to his side. "Who knows anything anymore? I've seen people do a

10

lot crazier things than this. And for a lot less. Did they find any of the stuff she took?"

"Nothing. And they can't be positive she's the one who robbed the place since no one actually saw her coming out of the building. But then, why else would she run?"

"Sure is a shame," Wink added. "Whatever she took, it must have been mighty important for them to keep dragging down there. I mean, the body would float up in a day or two anyway."

"We'll probably get a rash of leapers now, too," I added. "Seems like a person jumps and the crazies start lining up. Remember that one guy that climbed up on the top girder and did a swan dive? God, what a mess."

As passing traffic on the bridge began to pick up speed, the marine boat below continued to sweep from one bank to the other in an effort to locate the woman's body. The running lights of the boat cast a mesmeric effect as they reflected off the dark shimmering water. Every now and then, a shout could be heard over the drone of the inboard engines. The slack draglines behind the boat would suddenly go taut as they snagged on an old tire or some other piece of debris that lined the bottom of the river.

11

"Yeah, all they gotta do is wait a day or two and she'll float up, sure enough."

2

Home for me at present is a huge, three-story boarding house at the south end of the beach. Located at the end of Archer Road, it is referred to by most islanders as the "barn."

There's a simple explanation for that. The place looks more like a barn than it does a house. But it's not a bad place to live, don't get me wrong. The rooms are nice and the outside is covered with those natural wood shingles that have kind of a bluish tint to them.

There are about five boarders living there in addition to myself. Three of them, two guys and a girl, are students at a nearby junior college. One guy works at a surf shop on the boardwalk and the second girl is a schoolteacher at the elementary school down the road.

Then of course, there's Aunt Hattie, the woman who has owned the place for as long as anyone can remember. With the exception of a few streaks, her hair is a dignified gray. And she's a feisty old lady for her seventy-odd years. Packed into a five-foot-seven-inch frame, she walks with a gait most find difficult to keep up with.

Hattie is largely responsible for my staying in Jacksonville. I had just graduated from my journalism school in Michigan and had decided to celebrate with a few weeks vacation in Florida. On the way to Ft. Lauderdale, I planned to visit some relatives here I hadn't seen in years. A few days turned into weeks and I heard a room was available at Hattie's for a reasonable price.

"Why in the world would you ever want to go back up north to work anyway?" she barked one day. "If you had any sense, you'd look around down here in the sunshine."

She certainly had a point, but it still didn't seem feasible. In any event, I drove into downtown Jacksonville and paid a visit to the managing editor of the *Chronicle*. One thing led to another and before long, I was working as a stringer and soon after, as a full-time police reporter.

For about a year, I lived in a small bedroom on the first floor near the kitchen and dining room. However, when the car salesman moved out, Hattie let me have his room on the third floor which overlooked the ocean. I've accused her of getting me to stay because she likes me. She insists it's because I pay the rent on time.

There are few things prettier than a sunrise over the Atlantic. Since I usually don't get home until well after midnight, I'm seldom up early enough to enjoy the spectacle. However, the morning after the incident on the bridge, I awoke around 6 A.M. and went for a run on the beach.

I try to run at least a mile every morning, right after my ritual cup of coffee. Since our place is situated on a fairly remote section of the dunes, I'm usually able to jog without much of an audience.

Coming in from the beach, I found Hattie sitting at the dining room table in her pink bathrobe, forcing down a cup of black coffee.

"Well, well. If it isn't the bionic beach-comber," she said with her usual sarcastic wit. "Still trying to get in the *Guinness Book of World Records*, I see."

"Not really," I replied. "Couldn't sleep so I figured I'd get a little exercise before it got too hot out there."

"You were out pretty late last night, weren't you? I don't remember the time but I was reading and heard you park that bomb of yours in the driveway."

"Yeah, I was out till about three or so," I replied.

14

"Go chasing the local minors again, did you?"

"Nope. Seems a woman jumped off the Andover Bridge last night, Hattie."

"Don't say. Not a very good place to go swimming," she said, shaking her head.

"Yeah, especially when you consider she jumped from about 150 feet," I added.

"Anybody we know?"

"No. I think her last name was Johnson but I'm not sure. Somebody said she was a secretary but they were still running down leads when we left."

"Do they think it was suicide?" she asked as she got up from the table and walked back into the kitchen for another cup of coffee.

"I don't know. They're pretty sure she was the one who broke into the museum, although they didn't find anything in her car. And she must have realized she didn't stand a chance jumping off the bridge."

After a shower and a couple of peanut butter sandwiches, I drove downtown to see if the detectives in homicide had turned up anything.

Lieutenant Ron Marler, who heads up the division, was going over some papers in his office when I walked in. His looks are a little deceiving. He is only about five-foot six-inches tall with a rounded, pudgy face.

However, he can be plenty hard-nosed when he wants to, which is a lot of the time.

"Have they found the body yet?" I asked.

"Nothing yet," he said, not bothering to look up from his papers. "However, I'm sure they've found every old tire on the bottom of that river by now."

It was early afternoon and the office was empty since most detectives were still on the street. After pouring a cup of the department's finest from a grimy Mr. Coffee maker located atop a nearby filing cabinet, I slid into a chair opposite Marler's desk.

"Who was she, Lieutenant?"

"Name was Vicki Johnson," he said. "At least, that's who the car was registered to. White female, twenty-eight years old. She apparently worked for a freight forwarding operation over on Meyer Street."

"What did she take from the museum?"

"I didn't say she took anything from the museum," he said, looking up from his papers to emphasize the point so as not to be misquoted. "However, I will say close to a million in jewelry was taken from the museum. Maybe she took it, maybe she didn't. We won't know until the body is found."

"I figured it was the Spanish treasure that was taken. We ran a story on it a couple of

16

days ago. It was part of the treasure recovered two years ago from that old galleon sunk off the Keys."

Marler looked up from his papers and stared with a certain annoyance. "Well, it looks like the treasure has gone back to the deep because we can't find any trace of the woman or the jewels."

"Maybe she dumped the stuff before she leaped off the bridge," I said.

"We thought of that, but the patrolman who chased her said he had her in sight almost the whole time and didn't see anything thrown out of the car."

The phone rang and Marler cradled the receiver against his shoulder as he doodled on a notepad.

"Well," he said, "that was marine and it seems they found some clothing down there that matches a description of what the Johnson girl was wearing last night."

"But no sign of the girl?"

"No."

"Last night, I noticed a tanker passed under the bridge about the same time as the incident. Have you checked with the Coast Guard yet?"

Marler leaned back in his chair and blew cigarette smoke at the fluorescent light overhead. "They caught up with them this

17

morning," he said. "They claim they didn't see a thing – no girl, no jump, no body – nothing."

"You don't suppose the whole scheme could have been planned around that ship, do you?"

"Naw," he sneered. "She still would have gotten busted up even if she jumped on the deck of the ship. And besides, they checked the boat over top and bottom and didn't find a thing."

"Just the same, I think I'll dig around a bit. What was the name of that ship?" I asked.

"Let me see. It began with an L..." he said, fumbling through the notes on his desk. "Yeah, the *Levkas*. That was the name of it. The *Levkas*. But don't tell anybody you got it from me, hear?"

"Right," I replied, tossing the styrofoam coffee cup in the trash can on my way out.

Workmen were replacing the glass door panels at the museum as I made my way past. The main lobby was large and spacious with long winding galleries on each side of the massive marbled hall. An announcement board near the entrance still proudly stated that the exhibit of the treasure taken from the Spanish ship, the *Santa Augustin*, was now available for viewing. In a little pocket at the bottom of the

18

board were mimeographed folders describing how the ship sank in a storm off the Florida Keys in 1625. It also told of the efforts required to find the wreck and salvage the treasure.

"Hi, I'm Brad Norris of the Jacksonville *Chronicle*," I said to a young woman with blond hair who happened to be walking by. "Could you tell me where I might find the manager?"

"I'm the manager – my name is Gail Tomlinson," she replied. "May I help you?"

"Yes, well, I was here last night after the robbery. Just thought I'd stop by this morning and see what was taken."

"Well, the insurance company is handling all of the details. Since all of the items were irreplaceable, it may be a while before they can put a dollar estimate on the loss." The slender, well-poised woman was dressed in an attractive brown tweed dress with an unusual gold emblem pinned to her white satin blouse.

"Were the items taken all part of the exhibit you had on display here?" In the center of the rectangular gallery to the left of the large hallway, were several display cases which had contained the stolen treasure. The glass panels of the cases had been broken out.

"Yes, I'm afraid so," she said, shaking her head. "The most valuable piece was a necklace carved from a single piece of gold. And attached to the necklace was a large diamond encased in solid gold."

"How much was it worth?" I asked, jotting down a few facts in my notepad.

"Your guess is as good as mine," she said. "There wasn't another like it in the world."

"Who owned the treasure?"

"It belonged to an outfit in St. Petersburg called Off Shore Divers, Inc. They were the people who discovered the old ship. Then, I understand, the state claimed that since it was discovered in Florida waters, a quarter of it was rightfully theirs. While his lawyers planned to fight the battle in court, the man who owns the company tried to meet expenses by taking the collection on tour."

"Do you remember his name?" I asked.

"I'm afraid I've forgotten," she said. "But I do know he wasn't handling the tour himself. I understand he'd turned the whole affair over to a public relations firm in Miami."

"I still can't understand how she could have gotten in here. Don't you have a burglar alarm system on that front door?" I asked.

"Uh, yes, but I really don't know any of the details about that," she said. "I'm afraid you would have to talk to the insurance people."

It seems a little strange they would have such a valuable collection on display with such little regard for security. But then, I couldn't remember any time when the city had hosted such an expensive showing. I figured this heist would just have to be chalked up to the prevailing small town mentality of the museum's security.

"Have you had a lot of people come to see the exhibit?"

"Yes, especially this weekend. Yesterday was the last day in Jacksonville. Two men from the museum in New Orleans arrived this morning to take the collection there for the next showing. I'm afraid we forgot to call them in the confusion of last night."

"You know, the thing that baffles me is why the girl jumped from the middle of that bridge," I said. "And what about the jewels? If a person was leaping to her death, I don't think she would worry about the jewels, do you? Were the items she took very heavy?"

"Not necessarily," Gail replied. "However, it probably would have taken both hands to carry it all. She must have had a sack or something."

"Yes, well, thanks for your time," I said, handing her one of my business cards. "If you learn of anything new would you call me?"

"Sure," she smiled. "I'll be glad to."

Leaving the museum, I stopped for a

cheeseburger and Coke. I arrived back at the newsroom shortly after 3 P.M.

If you've ever been inside the newsroom of a fairly large paper, then I don't need to give you a description. There is one cavernous room painted a pastel yellow, green or blue, with rows and rows of gray, government issue desks neatly aligned. And on top of each desk sits a battered Olympia typewriter. Toward the front of the room is the city desk which amounts to the room's nerve center. The rest of the linoleum-tiled space is taken up by reporters. The lower in pecking order a reporter is, the farther toward the rear of the room his desk is located.

And black dial desk phones, circa 1950s! You'd think since reporters spend so much time on the phone, they would at least have push button models. But then, any reporter will quickly tell you the last place a paper spends money is in the newsroom.

The *Chronicle* is a pretty large paper with a circulation of a little over 100,000. It has a nice layout and a good bit of money has been spent in updating the business. However, it's still a small town weekly at heart. Formed about a century ago, most of the competition died out long ago so that the paper enjoys a pretty comfortable monopoly on the local news. The television stations do a credible job

22

of covering the breaking stories, but for print journalism, the nearest competitor is at least an hour's drive in any direction.

City editor for the paper is Max Schuman, a short balding man in his mid fifties. Starting as a copy boy years ago, he worked his way up to his present job. Most of his time is spent on the phone. However, he gets tired of talking to interesting citizens with not so interesting news-tips and meanders through the newsroom, chatting with reporters whenever he can. One of his jobs is assigning general assignment reporters to cover certain social events. He is also the man responsible for determining what local news goes into the paper.

I am spared the drudgery of covering such events as garden parties since I'm a beat reporter. My job each day is to report any police related activities. Staying on top of developments in the Johnson case was one of those responsibilities.

"Heard you had a busy night last night," Max said as I checked my mailbox.

"Yeah, it was interesting all right. I stopped by the museum on my way in but didn't find much. The girl apparently knew what to go for. But her suicide is still a mystery – at least to me."

"What'd the cops have to say?"

"They don't know any more than I do. Or at least they're not talking," I replied.

"Well, I'm fixing to make up the budget for tomorrow's edition. How much of a story should I plan on?"

"It's good for at least twenty inches," I said. "Did Wink get any good pictures last night?"

"Not bad, but since your story is a day old and the pictures really don't show anything except an empty car, we probably won't use them. Let me know if you turn up any new developments."

"Right," I replied, walking toward my desk at the rear of the newsroom.

The offices of Mediterranean Maritime, Inc., were located in a white one-story concrete building down the street from the Port Authority docks. Inside, two secretaries labored over their electric typewriters and intermittently wrestled with the phones. Off to one side was the manager's office and in front of the doorway was an empty desk with a nameplate which read MISS JOHNSON. The walls were lined with various certificates and pictures of tankers and cargo ships the company represented.

Manager of the company was a tall thin man named Hall. He was dressed in a light gray checked suit with a white short-sleeve

24

Perma-Press shirt and dark blue club tie. His skin was white except for a maze of tiny blood vessels that highlighted his prominent cheekbones. He had narrow lips that hardly moved when he talked.

"Mr. Hall, I'm awfully sorry about your secretary. How long had Miss Johnson been employed here?"

"I don't remember exactly but I guess it had been about a year, perhaps a little longer," he replied, standing in the doorway of his small office.

"Was she a good employee?" I asked.

"Look, I'm as much shocked by her actions as anyone else. We've never had any kind of trouble here. Just a small company handling ship cargoes. Whatever she did had nothing to do with this company."

"I never said it did," I replied. "I didn't mean to imply that your company was in any way associated with this incident. I was merely curious as to why such a normal woman would suddenly steal a fortune in jewels and then jump off a bridge." Hall began to relax a bit and invited me into his office, offering a chair opposite his desk.

"She was a very competent secretary," he said, resting his bony elbows on the arms of his swivel chair and touching his fingertips together, forming a triangle with his hands.

25

"I'm afraid I don't know that much about her private life. She was single and rented an apartment somewhere on the eastside. I can look up the address if you like, but I don't think you'll find much there. I know she liked to spend her weekends out of town or at the beach whenever she could. Orlando, Tampa, Atlanta . . . she liked to get away, if you know what I mean."

"How about friends?" I asked. "Do you know any of the people she ran around with?"

"No, I'm afraid not. Vicki was a friendly and outgoing girl, but she did lead a personal life away from the office. You're welcome to talk with the other secretaries, Mr. Norris. However, I don't believe they would be able to add much."

"That's okay," I replied. "Did you have any idea she was planning the robbery? Any suspicious phone calls or anything?"

"None whatsoever. Vicki hadn't been late for work in months. The last time she was in the office, she was smiling as usual. No, I can't remember anything unusual about her conduct at all." The interview was briefly interrupted by a phone call.

"Just out of curiosity, Mr. Hall. What is it your company does?"

"We represent shipping companies throughout the Mediterranean who do

26

business in the United States," he replied. "Negotiate contracts, even load and unload the ships when they arrive in port. Most of our customers are from Italy and Greece although we do occasionally contract with companies in Israel."

"There was a cargo ship in port over the weekend called the *Levkas*," I said. "Did your firm handle them?"

"Yes, the *Levkas* is owned by the Olympic fleet which is headquartered in Levkas, Greece. They are one of our largest customers. Why do you ask?"

"Well, I'm sure it's coincidental but the ship was leaving port and heading out to sea just as the Johnson woman jumped off the bridge."

"Really? And you think there is some sort of connection?"

"Not really," I added, "but the idea had crossed my mind. However, I understand the Coast Guard boarded the ship later and didn't find anything."

"Mr. Norris, just what do you intend to write about all of this?"

"Well, sir, at this point I don't know. Just doing a little background work to see what I can dig up. Why?"

"Well, I hope you will be able to keep the Mediterranean name out of all this mess. I

27

mean, after all, just because she worked for us doesn't mean the company should suffer. Don't you agree?"

"Don't worry, Mr. Hall. I don't intend to mention anything that isn't directly related to the story."

Hall got up from behind his desk and began walking toward the open doorway, indicating our conversation was over.

"You must forgive me, Mr. Norris, but I'm afraid this has all been a tremendous strain on us. I hope I've helped you a little but if you have more questions, perhaps another time."

"Thank you," I said. "By the way, would you have a list of the crewmembers of the *Levkas?*"

"No, only the captain of the ship would have that information. But I'll have one of the girls get it for you and call your office," he said, closing the door behind me.

It was late in the afternoon and thunderclouds were beginning to build up west of the city.

3

There are only two colors in the Florida Keys – blue and green. That is, of course, unless you count the hundreds of shades in between. Or the sugar-white sand that covers the islands and rushes down from the dense vegetation to greet the pounding surf of the Gulf Stream.

After a refueling stop in Naples, Fla., Hattie and I flew due south in the borrowed Cherokee Piper at an altitude of 10,000 feet. Our destination – Key West, or the "rock" as it is called by the islanders. At an airspeed of one hundred twenty knots, it is a little less than a two hour flight.

Almost a week had passed since the incident on the bridge. I had tried to get in touch with the owner of the diving company – a man named Adolf Furman. However, his secretary in St. Pete said he and several of his crew were taking advantage of the good weather and doing some diving at the wreck site.

Turning over new leads surrounding Vicki Johnson's death proved to be an exercise in futility. Since I had some vacation-time coming, I decided to combine a little business with pleasure and pay Mr. Furman a visit on his own territory. Hattie decided to go along with the idea of doing a little shopping while I did a little snooping.

The single-engined Piper belonged to one of the guys in marketing who leased out the plane when he wasn't using it. Flying was one of the few useful things I picked up in college ROTC. However, I hadn't kept up with it as much as I should have because of the high price of fuel.

"Is that Key West on the horizon?" asked Hattie, pointing over the cowling of the airplane. I nodded. Turning the radio to the frequency of 118.2, the Key West International Control Tower, I could make out the chatter of a few airplanes in the area. The emerald green island lay fifty miles in front of us. It was a beautiful day for flying. A few puffy clouds hung suspended in a vast expanse of rich bluish hues. Below, we would occasionally spot the outline of a sloop on its way to the island's port or the silhouettes of wandering sharks and porpoises as they swam about in search of food.

My aged and entertaining landlady had been quiet for most of the four-hour trip. We had left Jacksonville early in the morning and with the exception of a few brief conversations concerning weather and location, most of her time had been spent gazing out over the wing as the tropical Florida landscape passed beneath.

Her light brown skin was wrinkled from exposure to the harsh sun. Her tiny straight nose served as a perfect balance to her small rounded face.

Hattie never married, but had devoted thirty-five years to teaching high school students the rudiments of English literature. Life was certainly good to Harriet Blackwell – she would be the first to inform you of that. Despite her age, she still enjoyed the optimistic and enthusiastic spirit of a teenager.

"Key West approach, this is Cherokee November four-eight-two-five Bravo," I said, keying the microphone.

"Acknowledged, two-five Bravo," came the reply through the tiny speaker located in the ceiling panel to the left of my head.

"We are approximately twenty-five miles out approaching from the northwest. Request landing instructions, over?"

"Roger, two-five Bravo. There's a Cessna Skyhawk about fifteen miles ahead of you. Turn to a heading of one-five-zero and maintain an altitude of at least 2,000 feet. Winds are out of the west at nine knots. Runway in use is two-seven."

31

"Roger approach," I replied, securing the mike on the dashboard hook.

Hattie's blue cotton summer dress was beginning to show a few wrinkles from the morning of cramped confinement in the tiny cockpit. I was glad to see the creases of weariness in her face were starting to disappear as the skyline of the small tourist city grew larger on the horizon.

"Should be a fun weekend," I said. Adjusting the trim tab, the plane's nose dipped slightly and began a very gradual descent in altitude.

"Well I should hope so. At least I'm going to have fun. I don't know about you – probably be off spying around on that diving company or whatever it is you came down here to do."

"Doesn't hurt to ask a few questions, Hattie. And besides, if I can get anything out of it, maybe I can write some of this off on my expense account."

At first impression, Hattie's personality was one of abrasiveness. She seemed like a sarcastic old dame to strangers. But to those who knew her well, she was a sweet old lady beneath the gruff exterior.

After vectoring around to the far end of the island and securing permission to land, we made a sweeping arc and approached the airport from the southeast. Located on the southern end of the island, the runway is parallel with Smathers Beach and Roosevelt Boulevard. Off the left wingtip was the East Martello Tower, an old red-brick Civil War fort since converted into an art museum and gallery. Just 90 miles to the south was the island of Cuba and the port city of Havana.

I pulled back on the throttle and eased back slightly on the yoke, giving the plane a slight flair. The main wheels squealed as they gripped the hot asphalt of the runway.

The city had changed little since my last trip there two years before. The island of almost 30,000 people enjoys a strange dichotomy. Established early in the 19th century, it existed as a relatively unknown fishing village until Hemingway and Harry Truman put it on the map. Prior to World War II, the only ways of getting to the place were by boat or train. Many of the two-story wooden houses with the gingerbread trim had since been replaced with modern concrete and glass. The true flavor of the slow easy lifestyle has been eradicated by the fancy tourist hotels and those perennial "Conch Trains" that snake through the streets in every direction.

However, in parts of the four-mile long city, especially in the older sections and along the waterfront, some of the old style buildings painted in the pastel shades of pink and blue still remain. A dying breed perhaps, but far from extinct.

We quickly loaded our baggage into a nearby cab and sped across town to the opposite end of the island and the Casa Bahama, an elegant hotel at the foot of Margaret Street.

"Good afternoon, Mr. Norris," said the desk clerk at the hotel. "We've been expecting you. The bellhop will show you to your rooms. Hope you enjoy your stay," he said, handing over the keys.

The Casa Bahama is a relatively new three-story hotel although the exterior is a faded pink in the traditional style of the island. Our rooms were located on the second floor of the U-shaped building, overlooking the swimming pool and outdoor patio situated in the courtyard. Peering through the glass door and over the small balcony, I had little trouble making out the beautiful forms of several bikinis lounging poolside.

Margaret Street is a narrow strip about five blocks long and located in the older section of the city. The southern end of the street begins at the old city cemetery and runs past the shops and restaurants, eventually leading to the city's old docks known as the Key West Bight. This is where most of the islanders who still fish or pursue the monstrous sea turtles for a living moor their boats. It was also the place where I had been told Furman kept his salvage ship, the *Reef Runner*, whenever it was operating out of Key West.

"Well," said Hattie through the door that separated our adjoining rooms, "I believe I'll walk over to Mallory Square and do a little shopping. Care to come along?"

"Thanks, but I believe I'll go for a little walk down by the pier," I replied.

"Haven't even unpacked and you're already playing Lou Grant," she said, shaking her head. "I can see you're not going to be much company on this trip."

"Not true," I pleaded. "Just plan to ask a few questions and then spend the rest of my weekend sitting by that pool down there." I sneaked another peek to make sure my potential friends at water's edge had not left.

"Suit yourself. Just don't go home without me."

"Deal," I replied.

The shops along the wharf are probably much the same as they were a hundred years ago. All unpainted weathered wood hammered together with even less effort spent on refurbishing the interiors. However, the unique appearance of this run-down area probably induces the tourists to leave behind more of their money. Lots of little craft shops – leather, candles, and trinkets of every size and dimension. On every block is a restaurant with a screen door and some gently spinning ceiling fans, revolving padded stools and the remains of a chocolate cake encased in a plexiglass dome at the end of the counter. Their specialties are always turtle soup or pie – something made out of the reptile meat. There is even a large demand for the lacquered shells for some unexplainable reason.

The *Reef Runner* was backed into its slip, floating quietly in the afternoon sun. The slip was located about halfway down the pier, in front of a little Cuban deli indentified only by a crude handpainted sign which stated simply, CAFE.

The boat appeared much as I expected it would. Approximately sixty feet long, its overall design fell somewhere between a shrimper and a tugboat. Several coats of exterior marine white paint covered the weathered wooden hull which sat low in the water. There was a rather small bridge toward the front of the boat with a spiral staircase inside leading to a lower deck containing crew quarters and galley. A large portion of the rear deck was open to accommodate air compressors and the like. The only sign of activity on board was a tall slender brunette waxing the mahogany woodwork on the open deck.

"Hello," I said from the pier next to the gangplank. "Can you tell me where I might find Mr. Adolf Furman?"

"Yes, he's down below," said the brunette with a nice smile. "But I'm afraid he has a reporter with him at the moment. Was he expecting you?"

"No, I'm afraid not. My name is Brad Norris and I'm a reporter from Jacksonville. I've been investigating the theft of the *Santa Augustin* treasure last week and I understand you folks were the ones who found it. I was hoping Mr. Furman would be able to tell me a little about the treasure."

"I see," she said, turning the wiping cloth in her hands. "If you'll wait a moment, I'll tell him you're here."

I tried to look uncomfortable standing there on the dock in hopes the girl might invite me aboard. However, she apparently didn't take notice of my awkwardness for she turned and walked toward the wheelhouse. In a minute or two, a man of medium-sized build with little hair and a deep tan appeared from the front of the boat.

"I'm Adolf Furman. May I help you?" he said, extending his hand to invite me aboard his boat. I wasted no time in slipping over the gangplank.

"Hello, I'm Brad Norris of the Jacksonville *Chronicle*. I decided to fly down for the weekend and get a little sun. And while I was here, I was hoping you could tell me a little about the treasure that was stolen last week."

"By all means," he smiled, gestured me toward the wheelhouse. "By coincidence, we happen to have another journalist on board. I hope you don't mind."

"No, that's fine with me," I said, wondering who else was working the story.

Furman had a pleasant face, an expression that I guess comes from constantly working in the outdoors and doing something you enjoy. As I said, he was almost bald and the top of his head had probably been sunburned so often it was permanently browned. He was wearing a pair of faded Levi's, striped polo shirt and tennis shoes which looked a bit odd for his age – I guess in his early fifties.

He directed me through the cozy control room of the ship and down the twisting metal spiral staircase and into the ship's galley below. The room was about fifteen feet long with a long wooden table running through the middle. The sides of the room were curved

38

with the shape of the hull and over the table hung two old-style kerosene lamps with large green shades reflecting the faint glow of the wicks. At the far end of the little dining room was an even smaller doorway which led to an anteroom containing a stove and refrigerator.

Sitting at the table was an attractive girl in her early twenties with long brown hair. Dressed in a light brown corduroy pantsuit, she was wearing a pair of large plastic hornrimmed glasses. And spread out on the wooden table in front of her were a couple of those little notebooks reporters like so much.

As Furman and I made our way down the winding staircase, the woman turned.

"Mr. Norris, this is Miss Rogers. She's from New York and has come down to do a story on our operations here," Furman said. "Would you like a drink? We have bourbon, vodka, or some rum, whichever you prefer."

"Thanks, but I'm a man of simple tastes. Do you have any beer?" I asked.

"I think there's a can or two left," he smiled. "Why don't you make yourself comfortable."

I slid behind the table next to the woman.

"I'm sorry but I don't believe I caught your first name."

"Tracy," she smiled. "And yours?"

"Brad," I replied.

"Well, it's nice to meet you, Brad."

"Likewise," I replied with a stupid grin. Furman to the rescue with a cold beer.

"Mr. Norris, I'm afraid your trip down here has been wasted since there is very little I can tell you," Furman said. "It's been over a year since we discovered most of that treasure and I haven't seen it since then. As for the robbery last week, I'm sure you know more about that than I do."

"So far, the police haven't got any leads on either the treasure or the girl," I said, sipping the cold beer. "It looks like the woman had them on her when she jumped and, with the exception of a few pieces of her clothing, no sign of the body."

"But surely they should have found something by now," Furman exclaimed. "After all, it has been more than a week!" The girl sitting next to me was making a few notes in her pad as I filled them in on the details of the bizarre theft.

"I talked with the woman at the museum in Jacksonville on Monday and got a general idea of what was taken," Furman said. "I assume she described the necklace to you. That was by far the most valuable piece in the collection. The rest, various rings and

40

bracelets were worth a lot but not nearly as much as the necklace."

"Was the whole thing insured for its full value?"

"Oh, hell yes. That was one of the requirements the state of Florida made prior to the beginning of the tour," he said, refilling his glass with an extra squirt of bourbon. "I couldn't tell you who was carrying the policy or how much it was actually worth. That was handled by the public relations firm in Miami; they set up the whole thing. But it was supposed to cover the treasure in case something like this happened. Since the state claimed partial ownership, they set up the requirements and we were obliged to comply. Seemed like a waste of money at the time but I'm awfully glad now."

"Yeah, I can imagine," I said. "But since they were one-of-a-kind items, won't the amount the insurance company pays off be considerably less than what the treasure is worth?"

"I'm sure it will. However, the state had the treasure frozen all this time while they tried to decide how much of it was rightfully theirs. That's why we took the whole mess on the road. This kind of an operation requires working capital and there was a good chance those pieces would be tied up in litigation for

41

years. I imagine the state will be willing to deal a little faster now that we're talking in dollars and cents."

"Well, maybe the cops in Jacksonville will get lucky and find the treasure," I said.

"Perhaps," Furman said. "According to the ship's manifest, there is still several million dollars worth down there. Our other boat, which is smaller than this one, is out there right now keeping an eye on the claim. We'll be going out tomorrow to do some diving. You're both welcome to come along if you like."

"Thanks, I appreciate that," I said. "Now, if you'll excuse me, I think I'll wander back to our hotel for a while. Thanks for the beer and the hospitality. I'll look forward to seeing you tomorrow morning."

"See you then," Furman said, escorting me over to the stairwell. "By the way, we usually eat breakfast in the cafe over there if you would care to join us in the morning. About 7 A.M."

The mid-afternoon sun was still beaming down on the throngs of tourists as I made my way topside. Since I hadn't eaten lunch yet, I went to the cafe across from the boat and decided to have a piece of cake from beneath the plastic cover at the end of the counter. It took only a few bites to realize that breakfast

42

in the morning would probably be better at the hotel than this Cuban-style beanery.

Back at the Casa Bahama, a check at the front desk found a note from Hattie:

Met some old traveling friends over at the square. Plan to eat dinner and talk over old times. Don't wait up – Hattie.

The prospect of eating dinner alone didn't sound so bad since the chocolate cake had pretty well destroyed my appetite. I changed into a pair of bathing trunks and quickly retired to a comfortable lounge chair poolside. The hot afternoon sun had driven away all but a few of the sun-worshipping die-hards. Some scraggly old palm trees were planted at each corner of the courtyard and at one end of the inner sanctum was a bamboo har with several padded stools and a smiling Bahamian bartender for the benefit of the hotel patrons.

After a couple of Margaritas on the rocks, the fatigue of the flight caught up with me and I fell asleep in the chair. When I awoke an hour or so later, the sun had begun casting shadows against the opposite wall of the hotel and Tracy Rogers, clad in a flattering black satin bikini, was reading a magazine in a lounge chair just a few feet away.

"Hi. I didn't realize you were staying at the hotel, too."

"They invited me to stay on the boat, which I did for a couple of days. But I had to have a shower I could move around in so I rented a room here yesterday. I guess I'm just not much of a seagoing person."

"How long have you been sitting out here?" I asked.

"About a half hour, I guess. You were snoring so loudly, I hated to wake you."

"Sorry about that," I said with a sheepish smile. "Furman have anything interesting to say after I left?"

"I should have left with you," she replied, putting down her magazine and sipping the remains of a Bloody Mary. "Just a lot of babble about his rags to riches success." Tracy had a cute smile and, although she was attractive in a pantsuit, she was absolutely stunning in her bikini.

"So you're doing a magazine feature on his operation, huh?" I asked. "Getting paid pretty well for it?"

"Not bad. About seven hundred for the story, and of course my expenses. And the bottom line of that amounts to a week's vacation in Key West. The article was a bargain, regardless of the amount."

44

"Can't argue with you there. Where do you live when you're not traveling?"

"New York, of course," she replied as if there was no other place to live. "I'm originally from Boston and went to school there but moved to the city when I decided to try and make it as a free-lancer. Most of the slicks have offices there and if you're going to pay the rent writing for those people you have to be there pitching when the decisions are made."

"Do you enjoy it?"

"Yeah, I guess so. There are a lot of easier ways to make a living, like digging a ditch or flying to the moon. Sometimes, nobody buys and I have to hit my father for a loan to stretch things out. But most of the time, I can stay ahead of the bill collector, which in this business may be termed a success. How about you? What paper did you say you write for?"

"Jacksonville *Chronicle*," I said, sucking on a remaining ice cube in the bottom of my glass. "I guess it's okay. Being a police reporter can get to you after a while, though. Always waiting for tragedy to strike – chasing ambulances all over town. Doesn't take long to become an 'adrenaline junkie,' as they say in the newsroom. You eventually reach the point where you're afraid to go to sleep at

45

night for fear some disaster will occur and you won't know about it.

"It really isn't bad when you're out there on the street and things are happening. I guess the worst part is after the story is written and things slow up a bit and you have all the time in the world to sit around and think about the crazy way you earn a living."

As we talked, the bright reds and pinks of the sunset gradually transformed into subtle shades of gray. The other sun-worshippers had abandoned the courtyard leaving Tracy and me to ourselves. She sat up in her chair and began looking for her flip-flops.

"Would you join me for dinner – that is if you don't have other plans," I asked. She gave me a coy smile.

"But I thought you were down here with someone else?"

"Just my landlady," I replied, "and she left a note saying she would be out with friends tonight."

"Well, okay then. It's a little before six now. Why don't you stop by my room about seven-thirty?"

My wristwatch showed 7:32 P.M. as I knocked on Tracy's door. She looked even better than she did on the boat or by the pool. Her long brown hair fell over her shoulders

46

and blended nicely with the light brown dress and jacket she was wearing. Very feminine and chic. Just the type of outfit one would expect to see on the streets of New York in the summer.

"You're late," she said with a grin.

"My how observant this journalist is," I replied. "Hungry?"

"Practically starving. Where are we going?"

"There's a nice little place called Grant's Garden over toward the Square that has some outdoor tables and great seafood."

"Great. I can hardly wait," she said, pulling the door of her room shut behind her. I think the city of Key West, like most cities, takes on a different atmosphere at night. The shadows of the street lights give a totally opposite impression than the light of day. The side streets leading to the restaurant were well-lit, casting shadows on the unique architecture of the wooden buildings.

Grant's Garden is located next to an old two-story brick warehouse that has since been converted into several boutiques. Bright yellow tablecloths covered the outdoor tables and went well with the green and yellow canopies over each table. The waiters were dressed in red tuxedoes. A black iron grating set in the high brick wall separated us from the pedestrians.

"You look awfully nice tonight," I said. "Rather unusual for a journalist, you know."

"Oh really? No, I didn't know. And why is that so unusual for a journalist?"

"Well, you know what they say about women in this business not exactly being the fairest of the sex."

"No, I hadn't heard that," she replied with a curious smile. "And just what do they say about men journalists?"

Scratching my head as if genuinely perplexed, I answered, "I don't believe any generalizations have ever been made about men journalists."

"There you are," she said, sipping from the glass of Cabernet. "I guess that indicates the gender which invented that myth, doesn't it?"

"I prefer to think of it more as an unscientific survey."

"Not to change the subject, but tell me, did you happen to see the *Augustin* treasure before it was stolen?"

"No, I'm afraid I didn't. But then I'm not what you would call an art freak. One of the writers from the woman's section did a piece on it about a week before. Why do you ask?"

"Just wondering. Do you think it possible

48

that somebody else could have discovered the body and found the jewels in the process?"

"Naw," I replied with a mouthful of the house salad. "Even if they found the body, they would have had to dispose of it somehow. And the police have been over every square inch of the river for five miles in both directions."

"But they could have put the body in their boat and taken it out to the ocean or something, right?"

"Umm, I suppose so. But the Coast Guard has kept a pretty close watch on river traffic. And the marine people were on the scene within half an hour after she jumped. If they couldn't find her, I doubt that somebody floating by would have. Unless they knew she had robbed the museum. Why drag a dead body into a boat? Why not just call the police. I mean have you ever seen the victim of a drowning? I sure wouldn't drag anything like that into my boat unless I was getting paid for it." Tracy waved her fork in my direction indicating that she did not wish to pursue the details of the case any further.

She added, "I don't profess to know as much about this sort of thing as you do. But isn't it possible that she could have been working with someone else on this thing? They could have been standing by to pick her up?"

"You mean pick up her body? The medical examiner said a person's chances of surviving a fall like that were probably about fifty-fifty. If she had been working with somebody else, I think they would have planned their escape a little better than that. No, there is just no way I believe she could have intended to jump off that bridge."

"How about a parachute?"

"Maybe," I shrugged. "Couldn't have been anything conventional, though. Wouldn't have had enough time to open and slow the descent in that short a distance. But then a specially rigged outfit might have worked. But it seems to me that the cop chasing her would have seen something. He told me he was at the railing about 40 seconds after she jumped and saw no sign of life whatsoever. Not even a circus act could have cleared the area that quickly."

"Perhaps not, but it seemed like a possibility."

A warm wind gently blew out of the northwest as we left the restaurant and walked slowly in the direction of the hotel. The older middle-class tourists in their outlandish vacation costumes had been replaced in the

50

twilight hours by the younger people who sat on the steps of nearby doorways or wandered south of the Square in the direction of Sloppy Joe's, the bar where Hemingway reportedly tipped more than a few. A steady procession of cars with out-of-state license plates cruised in a makeshift parade up and down the street, eyes peering intently over the dashboards in case they should miss any of the sights or sounds the city had to offer.

"Thanks for having dinner with me, Tracy. I enjoyed the conversation as well as your company," I said as she fidgeted with the key to her room.

"You mean you're not going to come in for a nightcap?"

"Well, it's kind of late and we'll be starting early in the morning."

"Okay, but you don't know what you're missing. I don't like to brag but I've gained a certain amount of notoriety for my abilities in the art of mixology," she said.

"May it never be said that I turned down the offer of such a talented woman," I said, following her into the room.

"If you'll take the ice bucket on the vanity down to the end of the hall and get some ice, I'll warm up the rum."

"I'll be right back," I said, running down the hall swinging the plastic pail. I had the distinct feeling morning would come too early.

4

Seagulls screamed overhead as the *Reef Runner* pulled away from its slip and headed west toward the Dry Tortugas. The twin diesel engines rumbled beneath the wooden deck and the propellers churned up the foamy green water behind the boat. It was a little after eight and most of the serious fishermen had already left port. The members of the crew scurried about the boat as Furman, Tracy and I stood in the wheelhouse drinking coffee from plastic mugs.

"I'm glad the two of you could join us," Furman said. "I think you'll find the trip most interesting."

Once clear of the harbor, Furman spun the large wheel and the boat gradually turned to a southerly heading.

"I've been in this business for ten years – ever since I left the Navy – and never grown tired of it. The excitement of hunting for treasure has never dulled one bit. Not a great business if you want to be rich, mind you. But then, a person doesn't need much to get by around here."

"How far off shore is the wreck located?" I asked.

"About twenty miles to the south and midway between Key West and the Tortugas. There's a reef out there that is hard to spot until you're almost on top of it. During the early 17th century, the Spanish ships passed this way from South America en route to Europe and would wash up on the reefs during storms. As a matter of fact, that's how the citizens of Key West first made their living. When a ship was sighted breaking up on the rocks, the islanders would row out in their boats and salvage what they could from the sunken wrecks. Of course, the heavier items sank quickly and, with tides, became lost in a matter of months."

Tracy stood to the side of Furman, looking a little peaked from the constant rocking motion of the boat. I handed her a sweet roll from a pile near the coffee urn in the back of the cabin thinking it might help to settle her stomach.

"Mr. Furman, I would imagine you and the others have been combing these waters for years. I really doubt there's much of anything left down there to find, wouldn't you agree?"

53

"On the contrary," Furman said. "We've only scratched the surface. There are no accurate records as to how many wrecks may be scattered in these waters but I think it's safe to say the amount of treasure down there would run into the billions."

The *Reef Runner* was cutting through the water at about 15 knots when the silhouette of Furman's other boat stationed at the work site became visible on the horizon.

"Most of your crew look like college kids," Tracy said. "Where do they all come from?"

Furman looked very comfortable standing there in his blue and red striped polo shirt, white slacks and sneakers. As he talked, he kept a hand on the wheel and continued to stare through the open windows of the cabin at the large mass of green water ahead. The other boat grew larger as we approached the site of the sunken *Augustin*.

"Very observant," he said. "Some of them are college students. And then some of the older ones are majors in marine biology or related fields who began working with us during their summer vacations. I guess they were bitten with the same bug for adventure as I was. After finishing school, they one by one came and joined the family. And with the exception of living expenses, their pay is determined by how much treasure we find.

We share in the wealth and suffer together through the lean times."

A little strange, I thought. All these people so happy to be working for the sheer fun of it.

"How are times now?" I asked.

"In spite of the discovery of this treasure, we're still tight, what with the mess locked up in litigation and expenses and all. That's why we're hoping the insurance company will move quickly. I kind of doubt it considering the robbery and publicity this has gotten. But that's what we're hoping."

As we approached the other boat, I could read the name *High Time* painted on the transom in big gold letters. Furman cut the power and turned the wheel so our ship would float up alongside. Several tanned young men and women appeared from inside the smaller boat and made ready to secure lines between the two ships.

"Approximately twenty-two feet below us, Mr. Norris, lie the remains of the three hundred fifty-year-old ship with several million dollars worth of treasure in her holds. Now that must arouse at least a little excitement in you. And you, Miss Rogers?" Furman said, turning around to look at Tracy who was still standing behind him. She returned the smile, looking very

55

relieved that the pitching of the boat had finally stopped.

Several of the young crewmembers were already jumping over to the other ship as we walked to the side. One blond youth jumped across and landed right in front of us.

"This is Will Lambert, who's in charge of our diving boat," Furman said. "How's it been going, Will?"

"No problems, Mr. Furman. We had a crew down for about an hour this morning but didn't find much except for a few coins. We were just getting ready to go down again."

"Fine. Go ahead and we'll join you in a minute." Several of the men on the rear deck of the other boat were already slipping into their wet suits and tanks.

"The strange apparatus you see on the transom is a specially rigged thing we use for clearing away the sand," Furman added, pointing toward the rear portion of the *High Times*. When we first came out here, the *Augustin* was under about eight feet of sand. Moving several tons of sand is no easy job so Will came up with the idea of putting the prop wash to good use. It blows the sand out of the way but leaves the treasure behind, a method that has saved us countless hours of time and money."

We made our way over to their ship as three

of their divers slipped over the side and slowly disappeared into the green water's depths. About three minutes later, Lambert started the ship's engines so the workmen below could begin the tedious process of clearing away the sand.

"For every moment of excitement in finding treasure, there are hours of drudgery," Furman said. "It's like looking for the needle in the haystack. Only first, you have to find the haystack."

After about forty minutes, the divers returned to the surface and Furman was the first to greet them as they bobbed like buoys off the transom.

"What did you find?" he hollered at them.

"Quite a few more coins and a bracelet. We must be getting close to some more good stuff," said one of the divers.

"Excellent," replied Furman. "Help them aboard. Somebody turn off the engines."

Once aboard, the results of the dive to the bottom were spread out on the wooden rear deck of the *High Times*. There were thirty or forty coins, most of which were heavily encrusted with barnacles and the like. Also, a copper bracelet badly tarnished and covered with marine organisms. Perhaps a half-dozen small stones that looked like rubies were set in the bracelet. As Furman and his

57

crew sat on the deck, examining their find, Tracy moved around the group with her 35 millimeter Nikon, shooting pictures she would eventually use in her magazine article.

"Once polished, this will be a beautiful piece, although not worth more than perhaps $25,000," Furman said, turning the corroded item over in his hands. "Whenever a lot of pieces are found concentrated in one area like this, it's usually a good sign that more will be found. My theory is that these items were stored in a wooden chest which has long since rotted away, although the treasure generally remained in the same place."

"You estimate there's still a couple of million dollars worth of jewels down there. Did the list indicate what form the treasure was in?" I asked.

"Yes, mostly in currency. However, the manifest also listed other pieces of jewelry like the necklace. Combined, they might weigh a little over ten pounds. But in dollar value, they account for almost a third of the treasure," Furman said as he scraped away some of the crustations on the coins with his fingernail.

The crew of the *High Times* made two more dives after taking a short break for lunch. There were about a dozen men and women in their early to mid twenties who made up the crew of the work ship. They all seemed equally proficient at the many jobs required on board the vessel. While three divers worked on the ocean bottom at the wreck site, the others busied themselves topside, moving hoses, operating generators and tagging the discovered treasure.

It was shortly after 4 P.M. when Furman gave a short blast on the boat horn, indicating the end of the work day. The crew scurried about and in no time had all the salvage equipment neatly stored away. Tracy and I were standing with Furman on the bridge of the *High Time* when I noticed several of the college-age crew gathering at the stern of the ship.

"These kids work awfully hard," Furman said as he noticed me watching the crewmembers. "And when the day is over, they believe in having a good time. I hope the two of you don't embarrass easily."

Tracy glanced at Furman, wondering what he meant by the statement. However, before she could speak, she realized what he was referring to. As we watched, the crews of both ships began stripping off their clothes and jumping into the water naked. The air was filled with the sound of their laughter and giggles as they swam about, played tag and climbed back on board the ship to dive into the water again. They were all in very good shape with very nice tans. I tried to hide my delight in watching the beautiful coeds as they strutted around on the stern of the ship.

"Do they do this all the time?" Tracy asked as she stared at the naked crowd through her large hornrimmed glasses.

"Yep. But really, why not? They're not about to offend anybody out here. And although it may seem a little odd to you, they're all like brothers and sisters. After all, they put in long hours out here and life can get a little boring after a while."

"Evidently," Tracy said with a grin. "We should all be so lucky." As she spoke, she unconsciously felt her satin bikini to make sure it was still in place.

"You kids are more than welcome to go down and join them. I think you'd enjoy it if you gave it a chance."

At first, I didn't think much of the idea. But the more I looked at the coeds bouncing around on the back of the boat, the more I liked the idea. "What do you say, Tracy?" I asked.

"Thanks, but I believe I'll sit this one out," she replied.

"Now that's a fine way for a journalist to

act," I said in a mocking tone. "Where's your sense of adventure? And who knows. You could probably turn this experience into a good story."

"Thanks, but I think I'll let this one go. But don't let me stop you."

"Why don't you at least keep me company and go in with your suit on?"

"We'll compromise," she said. "I'll walk with you to the rear of the boat."

I didn't exactly run down the steps to the rear of the boat. Most of the others were in the water and didn't seem to notice Tracy and me standing nearby. Just thinking about it was actually worse than slipping off my trunks. I tried to do it as gracefully as possible but my foot caught in one of the leg holes. And Tracy staring at my body didn't help me to relax any.

I wasted no time jumping over the transom and into the cool water. It felt refreshing as I paddled away from the rear of the boat. It was the first time I had ever done anything like that. The swirling water felt strange but nice.

"Fun, huh?" asked a girl swimming nearby with large breasts and blond hair tied up in pigtails. She had one of the prettiest smiles I had ever seen. Funny how it's the smile I remember best.

"Yeah, feels great," I replied, trying to concentrate on baseball. A fraternity brother in college told me it is a surefire remedy to think about baseball when you're trying to conceal your excitement.

"Aren't you the reporter down here from Jacksonville?" she asked.

"Yes," I gurgled, trying to keep my head above water. As I dog-paddled in an effort to keep from drowning, I felt something brush against the inside of my legs. I also felt something pinch me on the butt.

"Hi," said a familiar face as it surfaced a few feet in front of me. It was the girl I had seen the day before polishing the railing of the ship. "You know, you're kind of cute ... all over," she said with a grin. I could feel myself blushing a little.

"Thanks. You're not too bad yourself."

"My name's Candy. What's yours?"

"Brad. I must admit I've taken a liking to your exercise period."

"When you spend as much time at sea as we do, you really have to work hard at finding entertainment."

"Well, you seem to be doing a pretty good job."

"You'd be surprised," she said, paddling a little closer towards me. "After a while, we all become pretty good friends out here. That's

62

why we enjoy visitors so much. New meat if you know what I mean."

"Yes, I believe I do."

Our conversation was interrupted by the rest of the crew who began an improvised game of "keep away" with a frayed volleyball someone had secured from below decks. I become so involved in watching the game, I almost missed noticing Tracy swim up beside me. The water was so clear, I had no trouble noticing she was also without benefit of clothes. It was actually the second time I had seen her naked. I don't know why but her body looked much more beautiful to me in the water than it had the night before.

"I would definitely feel more relaxed at this if you'd try not to stare," she said, swimming up to my side.

"What, and miss all the fun? No deal," I replied. "Swim near me and you'll have to put up with my lewd behavior."

"Well, it can't be any worse than last night," she said.

"I thought you had a good time last night."

"I did," she replied. "Just kidding."

After watching the crew toss the ball around for a few minutes, Tracy and I swam back to the transom and held onto the ladder in order to catch our breath. When Tracy began to shiver, I got around behind her and put my arms around her body to keep her warm. Her soft flesh felt awfully good. I hoped the moment would never end but it did.

Once back on board the *High Time* and into our clothes, we helped ourselves to large glasses of a special rum punch concocted by Furman and settled into a cozy spot by the ship's railing. Gradually, the crewmembers climbed on board to relax and sample the rum. Before long, a tall youth with sun-bleached hair produced a guitar and the crowd sang every song he could play at least twice. The sun had dropped to the horizon before the young crewmembers began slipping below decks to help prepare the evening meal. Tracy and I remained behind, holding each other as the sun turned the sky a brilliant red before slipping from sight.

"I wonder how many people through the centuries have watched the sun set from this very spot," Tracy said.

"I imagine the crew that sailed the ship beneath us would have been glad to forego the experience," I said.

"Very funny. But you know, this was a main trade route between South America and Europe. Doesn't it give you goosebumps to think that pirates sailed in these waters?"

"I suppose so," I replied. "But then, they

still do. I did a story a couple of months ago about how many boats are hijacked down here every year. Owners disappear without a trace and the ships turn up scuttled on some Godforsaken island. The Coast Guard doesn't like to talk about it. But from the people I talked to, it's apparently quite a problem."

"What do they take them for?" Tracy asked.

"The ships? A variety of reasons, I guess. But the main reason is to smuggle drugs into the country. It's easy to follow a freighter approaching Florida. But these waters are full of small boats. The Coast Guard can't begin to check them all. The perfect cover for the small-time smuggler."

Tracy shivered slightly. "I wish you hadn't told me that, Brad. Now, I don't think I'll be able to sleep tonight."

"You needn't worry, Tracy. I doubt if any smugglers will try to take over this boat considering all of the people on board."

"Say, are you kids hungry?" Furman asked as he appeared from the door of the wheelhouse. "Got some pretty good food down there and just enough left for you two."

"Sounds great," I said, getting to my feet. "We were just admiring the sunset."

"Know what you mean," he said, staring

out over the water to the west. "Spent most of my adult life on the water. And I've never grown tired of it. I still enjoy watching the sunset as much as I did when I was half your age. For beauty, I don't think there is anything that quite matches the sea."

As I stood there watching the last rays of sunlight reflecting off the water's surface, I began to realize how easy it would be for Furman to enlist the services of the college students who helped him. For them, money was of little value. It was the idea of adventure – hunting for buried treasure and ol' Davy Jones's locker that made it all seem worthwhile. I could even understand their almost blind loyalty to him. For many, he was probably the warm loving parent figure they never had at home. The thought of staying on the ship even appealed to me.

The Irish stew the crew had prepared for supper was very good. I don't know why but food aboard ship always tastes good to me. Maybe it's because at sea my allergies aren't quite so irritated.

After dinner, Tracy and I climbed up the spiral metal staircase that led to the deck and snuggled up on a mattress to enjoy the night air. There was barely a cloud in the sky and the heavens were filled with thousands of twinkling stars. Just enough of a cool breeze

66

blew across the deck of the *High Time* to make it all comfortable.

"Looks like you two have become pretty good friends," Furman said, kneeling next to Tracy and myself.

"Don't you know how journalists stick together? Safety in numbers," I said.

"More the romantic influence of the sea," Tracy added.

"My wife never cared much for the water," Furman said, removing the cellophane wrapping from a long, narrow cigar. "We divorced ten years ago. Couldn't hardly get her to set foot in a boat. Never could figure out why. She could swim. Just never took a liking to it."

"That's too bad," I said, trying to be polite. "Do you have any children?"

"A boy and a girl," he said, striking a match and lighting the cigar. "My daughter is married with two boys and lives in Atlanta. My son, he's a senior at the University of Florida. Plans to be an architect."

"What? And not go into the salvage business with you?"

"God, I hope not. I wouldn't wish this on anybody."

"I don't know why. Seems like you have a pretty nice life out here."

"Sure, the kids got it nice. They don't have

67

to worry about paying the bills and trying to keep these old tubs from sinking. But I can assure you, there isn't a lot of money in looking for sunken treasure. We get by and that's about it. If I didn't love the sea so much, I wouldn't bother with it."

"I could say the same thing about writing. Most people think journalists are paid a lot of money. But the truth is, most make very little when you consider the long hours they're forced to work."

"How come?" Furman asked.

"Shows like *Lou Grant*," I replied. "All of a sudden, everybody wants to be a journalist and the colleges start cranking out about 60,000 graduates a year. It's a buyers' market and the newspapers can get away with paying just about anything they want."

"Same holds true for magazines but not quite as bad," Tracy said. "The people with talent can still do pretty well. But then you never know when the next article is going to sell. Seems like it's always feast or famine."

"I sure hope the cops in Jacksonville can locate some of that treasure, Brad, or it is going to be famine around here for some time to come," Furman said.

"We can keep our fingers crossed," I said. "But it's been my experience if they can't get a lead in the first few hours, the chances are greatly reduced. But they may get lucky, you never know."

The end of Furman's cigar grew bright red in the darkness as he inhaled. "You just can't imagine the personal attachment for something like that treasure," he said, blowing the gray smoke in a steady stream from between his lips. "Sure, the money is important. But the time! I spent over five years poring over old Spanish maps before we ever started looking. And it took almost another year and a half before we even located the wreck site. No, it's more than the money. That treasure was a part of my life. I just can't believe it's gone like that."

"I wouldn't worry. It'll turn up sooner or later. My personal opinion is the woman panicked and pitched the jewels before she ever got to the bridge. The cops have staked out most of the pawn shops and fences in the area. Sooner or later, someone will try to sell a piece of it."

"Let's hope you're right, Brad. If we don't get some income pretty soon, I'm going to have to sell these ships."

"Can't you get some relief from the state?" Tracy asked.

"Naw, they've washed their hands of the whole thing. We even tried to get them to put some pressure on the insurance company to try and get them to pay off. But the people in Tallahassee wouldn't budge. No, it doesn't look like anybody is going to move on this thing and we're the ones who're going to suffer." Furman flipped the remains of his cigar over the ship's railing and got to his feet. "Well, I've got some paperwork to attend to below. The sky's clear. A good night to sleep under the stars."

"Yes, I think we'll stay up here for a while," I said.

"Holler if you need anything," he said, disappearing into the wheelhouse. Both ships were dark except for the running lights and a soft map light on the bridge. The sounds of the crewmembers singing in the galley to the accompaniment of the guitar player drifted up through the planking. A young couple standing on the bridge were the only other people topside. Tracy and I stretched out on our backs and stared up at the starry night.

"I sure hate to go back to work," I said.

"When do you leave, Brad?" Tracy asked, her hands clasped together beneath her head. She was still dressed in her bikini but had borrowed a loose-fitting sweatshirt from one of the women on board.

"Tomorrow morning. Soon as we get back to Key West."

"Will you keep in touch?"

"Sure," I replied.

"I've enjoyed the last twenty-four hours with you, Brad," she said, rolling over against my side and propping herself up on one elbow.

"You're a lot of fun, Tracy. We'll keep in touch." Feeling her breasts through the sweatshirt, I realized she had removed the top portion of her bikini. The realization conjured up images of her beautiful body underneath. She had a great body in addition to a sharp mind and a pleasing personality. Women of her caliber are not easy to find. If she lived closer to Jacksonville, I could see me falling for her in a big way.

"That's it?" she asked. "Just a lot of fun? I mean, didn't you feel anything last night?"

"Besides you?"

"No Brad, I'm being serious."

"Last night was something very special, Tracy. You're very special." I obviously said the right thing as she smiled and kissed me on the lips for the longest time.

"Have you ever thought of moving to New York, Brad?"

"New York? What would I do there?"

"I don't know. Write for one of the newspapers. Do a little free-lance, maybe."

"Not me, Tracy. I was born and raised in the Midwest. I'd be lost in a place like New York. I'm afraid I'm not much of a city boy."

"Aw, you'd love it," she said with a giggle as she slipped her hand under my jacket and rubbed my chest softly. "The theater, the museums, dinner at Sardi's. It's a writer's town, Brad. It never sleeps."

"Maybe it doesn't but I do. I don't think I'd like a steady diet of that, Tracy."

"Don't knock it till you've tried it."

"To tell you the truth, Tracy, I kind of enjoy Jacksonville. Granted, it's pretty short on culture. But I live on the beach, away from the bustle. A great view of the ocean. And I like a little land around me – plenty of room to breathe. You know what I mean?"

"We've got Long Island."

"Maybe. But I've always gotten the impression people live a little too fast up there for my taste. Think I'll stick to the south for a little while longer."

"Can't blame a girl for trying," she said, kissing my neck and ears.

"Not at all," I said. "As a matter of fact, I kind of like your style of persuasion."

"You sure are oversexed, aren't you?" she said, massaging my shoulders.

"Hey, you can't blame this all on me. You had a hand in getting me started," I said, rubbing her back beneath the sweatshirt. Her skin felt warm and good.

"Two hands, I'd say," she giggled.

I noticed out of the corner of my eye that the couple on the bridge had disappeared from sight. We were apparently the only ones on deck.

"Tracy, what do you say? Let's go downstairs for a little intense huggin'."

"What's wrong with right here," she sighed.

"What if someone comes up," I asked. "That could get a little embarrassing."

"Not if we pull this blanket over us."

I'm not exactly what you would call an exhibitionist. But Tracy had given me the choice of making love on the open deck or not at all. And to be honest, I found the thought of getting caught in such a loving embrace rather exciting once I got into it.

Tracy and I held each other beneath that blanket for a long time. I believe I could have remained in that position forever, had it not been for the wood planking of the ship's deck which was leaving rather painful imprints on my backside.

"Are you going to miss me?" she cooed,

73

rubbing her soft, supple body against mine.

"Why don't you move to Jacksonville?" I asked.

"Oh, Brad, I wouldn't be any happier in Florida than you would be in New York. I think we're going to have to settle for our occasional romantic interludes."

"That's not going to be easy. You're quite a woman."

"And you're one hell of a man," she said, rubbing her index finger lightly over my lips. "One thing New York doesn't have enough of is men like you."

"Maybe I should move there after all," I teased.

"You do and I won't let you out of my sight."

"Is that a promise?"

"Promise," she smiled.

The noise from below was gone and the ship was now silent. The only sound to be heard were the waves as they lapped against the gently rocking ship. It was a beautiful night. The last thing I remember before falling asleep was looking into Tracy's big eyes as hers gazed into mine. And I remember thinking at the time how glad I was that I had decided to fly down to Key West for the weekend.

5

Hungry seagulls circled noisily overhead as the *Reef Runner* chugged slowly within sight of Key West. The sun shone brightly and the air had a fresh, clean smell to it. I stood by the railing near the bow, drinking a cup of coffee and watching the white churning water as it broke beneath the bow of the large lumbering ship.

"Good morning." I turned to find Candy, the pretty young brunette, standing behind me.

"Hello again."

"Did you sleep well?"

"Yes, thank you. We slept on deck last night. The view was nice although I must admit the bed was a little hard."

"Doesn't get any more comfortable with time. I hope you've enjoyed your stay aboard ship."

"It's been very interesting. I've learned a lot about hunting for buried treasure," I said, sucking the last few drops of coffee from the bottom of my styrofoam cup.

"There's a lot more to it than most people imagine."

"How long have you been doing this – working for Furman, I mean."

"This is my second summer," she said, leaning against the railing. "I'm a senior at Florida Atlantic University, majoring in oceanography."

"Interesting. What do you plan to do when you graduate?"

"Haven't really decided yet. I may come back and work for Mr. Furman for a while until I make up my mind."

"You really enjoy it here on the boat?"

"Sure. We're all like a family. And Mr. Furman is the greatest. I mean, he really cares about us – what happens to us."

"From what he said last night, he may be in trouble financially if they can't find the stolen treasure or if the insurance company doesn't pay off."

"Yes, I know. Hurricane season will be on us soon. And Mr. Furman said we may not be able to come back if something doesn't happen. I sure hope they can find those stolen jewels. Do you think they will?"

"I wish I could say but you never know. Sometimes they get lucky and sometimes they don't."

"Gail Tomlinson said she didn't think they will," the young woman said.

"Oh, you know Gail?" I asked. Candy

suddenly got a funny look on her face as if she had spoken out of turn.

"Uh . . . no. I heard her name mentioned but I don't know her personally. She . . . umm, doesn't she run the museum in Jacksonville?"

"Yes," I said, realizing she was covering up something.

"I must have heard Mr. Furman mention her name."

"That's possible," I replied. "I know he said he talked with her last week."

"Yes, well, that's probably it. In any event, I hope they can find the treasure. Will you write us and keep us posted on how things are going?"

"I'll do what I can."

After going below to clean up a bit and change clothes, Tracy joined us on the ship's foredeck. The attractive crewmember stayed for only a few minutes before excusing herself and disappearing.

"You look nice, Tracy," I said.

"You *are* sweet. But I feel a little stiff from sleeping on that hard deck last night."

"You'll have plenty of time for rest once you get back to New York." She pouted slightly at the thought of returning home.

"When do you leave, Brad?"

"As soon as I can get back to the hotel and

77

gather up Hattie and the luggage. I need to get back to Jacksonville."

"I'm going to miss you, Brad," she said, rubbing the small of my back. "Sure you don't want to come to New York?"

"Not at the moment," I replied. "But don't hold me to it. I can always change my mind."

"Do you plan to write a story when you get back?"

"Yeah, I'll probably work up a feature about looking for sunken treasure. At least, I can write off part of the expenses that way. Too bad I didn't get any clues on the stolen loot."

"Maybe the police will know something when you get back."

"I doubt it," I said. "Although I did find Candy, the girl who just left, rather curious. I know she knows the woman who runs the art museum. But she went to great lengths to hide the fact. The big question is why." As we talked, I looked up at the bridge and could make out the face of Furman watching us through the big glass panels of the cabin. He certainly seemed like a nice enough man. But then I had learned in my short time as a newspaperman that you can't judge a person by his appearance. It is often the nice-looking guys that turn out to be the biggest crooks.

"I don't plan to put much about the stolen

treasure in my story," Tracy said. "But if you turn up anything, would you let me know so I can update it?"

"Sure," I replied. "At my usual rate, of course."

"I'll be glad to pay your rate anytime."

Furman backed the salvage boat into its slip at the dock and the crewmembers began throwing lines to people lining the wooden pier. I wondered if people who lived in the small city found it as exciting as those who merely visited. Even paradise can become a little commonplace, I guess.

"Thanks for the hospitality, Mr. Furman," I said. "The trip was most informative."

"I'm glad," he replied, extending his hand. "I'd appreciate a copy of any stories you write. And keep us posted on the search for the stolen treasure, okay? You can just call the cafe over there and they'll get word to us. Or call my office in St. Pete. Here's the number," he said, handing me a business card.

"I'll do that," I said, grabbing the overnight bag I had brought and stepping onto the gangplank. Tracy walked in front of me with a shoulder bag draped over her arm.

The crew of the ship was still busy securing lines and carrying supplies aboard as Tracy and I stepped from the pier and made our way up Margaret Street toward the Casa Bahama.

"When does your flight leave?" I asked.

"Not until four this afternoon. That gives me a little more time to sit by the pool and work on my tan."

"Wish I could stay to enjoy it with you but I really need to get back. And I'm sure Hattie will be ready to go."

"I understand," she said with a faint smile. "And after all, you promised to come visit soon. I intend to hold you to that promise."

After a few parting moments in Tracy's room, I returned to my own in order to pack and retrieve Hattie. She was downstairs in the gift shop buying a few postcards and searching for any worthwhile trinkets she might have overlooked.

It was after 2 P.M. by the time I got our baggage loaded into the Piper Cherokee and got the plane checked out and ready to go.

"Well, did you get what you came after?" Hattie asked once we were airborne and heading toward the mainland.

"And more."

"That good, huh? From the smile on your face, I'd say it must involve a woman."

"I did meet a very nice lady," I said. "She's a magazine writer from New York."

"That figures. I'm surprised she had anything to do with you. I thought all

80

those fancy writers from New York were pretty snooty."

"Not at all," I said. The thought of Tracy in my arms was still vivid. Perhaps I could talk Max into letting me go to New York for a good travel piece. Not impossible but highly unlikely.

6

Briiiiinnng!

The cool still darkness of the bedroom was interrupted by the phone. The clean sheets on the bed felt so good I never wanted to get up.

Briiiinng!

I would have jerked the damn cord out of the wall had I not been half asleep and the socket out of reach.

"Hello," I said in a barely audible voice.

"Brad, sorry to bother you but you've got to get dressed. The Ashton Hotel is on fire and it looks like a big one."

"Aw, have a heart, Max. We just flew in from the Keys a couple of hours ago. What time is it, anyway?"

"Nine in the morning. Look, I realize it's early but I can't spare any more day-side reporters and it's a three-alarm fire. So walk through the shower and get down there as fast as you can, okay?"

"All right," I replied begrudgingly. Walking half-dressed out the front door of the beach house and climbing into my '66 Mustang convertible, its seats still wet from the early morning mist, I made a mental note to look for more suitable means of employment at the end of the day.

Driving toward the city, I tried to remember everything I could about the old hotel that faced the city park. Built in the early 1900s, it was at one time considered one of the finest places to stay in the entire southeast. At the turn of the century, Jacksonville was the end of the line for the railroads as far as Florida was concerned. Wealthy folk from the East would come down for the winters, adding a considerable amount of prestige to the port city, not to mention the added dollars. By the 20s however, magnates like Henry Flagler began laying track to southern parts of the peninsula, building towns and diminishing the enticing lure of Jacksonville. That, and the trend following World War II of middle class citizens deserting the downtown area and running for the suburbs, had left the aging hotel to the winos and transients.

I thought back to a short feature I had

done on the hotel and its occupants about six months before. The once-plush carpets had since become dingy and worn in the well-traveled spots. And the years of dripping water faucets had left rust stains which had eaten away at the porcelain wash basins in the communal bathrooms at the end of each hall. Showers consisted of cold water, except in the winter when the pipes had a habit of freezing.

The Ashton was a victim of the 20th century and so were its residents, mostly old men in tattered clothes. A room there cost $18 a week or $3 a day. I remember the man at the desk telling me that about half of the tenants could only afford rent by the day.

And the men seldom lingered in the hallways of the building. They either stayed behind the locked doors of their room or watched the TV set with the bad reception in the lobby of the building. The stairwells of the building were a haven for young punks looking to steal the last few dollars a fella might have. And a closed elevator that only worked part of the time wasn't a great place to hang around either.

Although it was after nine, traffic on the highway leading from the beach to downtown Jacksonville was fairly congested. Driving around slow-moving cars and fudging on red lights, it still took almost a half hour to reach the blaze. Coming in on the Southside Expressway, I could make out heavy columns of black and gray smoke on the north side of the river. The Ashton was obscured from sight by several skyscrapers on the waterfront. However, I spotted several fire trucks from the south side of town heading over the Main Street Bridge with their lights flashing and sirens blaring.

I could still see clearly in my mind's eye those old wrinkled faces that I had interviewed in the hotel six months ago. Faces of men who had spent their lives going from one town to the next in search of the easy life. Chasing the rainbow. There they sat on their sagging metal beds, talking about the last town and this town and how things would be better in the next town.

All streets within a three-block area of the Ashton were blocked by the policemen, so I parked near the old theater and ran the three blocks to where police and firemen had set up a makeshift command post in a corner of the park across the street from the burning hotel. I recognized one of the fire chiefs as I approached.

"Chief, Brad Norris," I said, grabbing his arm in an effort to gain his attention. "How bad is it?"

"Well, we got three dead so far and the fire

is just about out," he replied, pulling his arm away and continuing to stare at the upper windows of the Ashton.

"How did it start?"

"Aren't sure yet. We think it may have started on the fourth floor. The third and fifth are so filled with smoke, our men are having a time getting in there." Looking up at the six-story concrete and masonry structure, I could make out the silhouettes of firemen in the windows as they raced through the rooms looking for traces of fire that might have burned through the upstairs flooring. Wink McCormick was standing in the street nearby, the electric shutter of his camera whirring as he snapped picture after picture.

"I understand they got three fatalities," I said to Wink. "Were you here when it happened?"

"Yeah, when the two guys jumped from the fourth floor," he replied. "I understand one guy burned to death up there. They haven't brought his body down yet."

"Where are the two that jumped?"

"They took 'em away about five minutes ago," he added, still aiming his 35 millimeter camera at the upstairs windows. "Both of them were old men, both white, who apparently woke up, smelled the smoke and figured jumping was the only way out. You better check with the cops over there for I say they were dead when I'm not positive."

"I already talked to the chief. He said there were three."

"They should be bringing that third dude out in a minute," Wink added.

Just then, the voice of one of the firemen upstairs called over the tactical frequency of his two-way radio and announced that they had succeeded in putting out the fire. Without stopping to ask permission, Wink and I ran into the lobby of the hotel.

The smoke was still so thick on the fourth floor of the building it was almost impossible to breathe. Walking by one room that appeared to have been burned worse than the others, we spotted several para-medics putting the badly burned body of an old man into a plastic body bag. Wink snapped a picture or two while I attempted to get a few notes.

"Any idea who he is?"

"No ... hey, you guys shouldn't even be in here. You're gonna have to get your information from the chief. And besides, we don't know anything yet."

"Okay," I said. "I'm not going to quote you, anyway. Just wanted to get some background stuff, you know. Burned pretty bad, wasn't he?"

"Yep," replied the rescue technician. As they slipped the body into the plastic cover, I noticed an unusual ring on the victim's hand. It looked like gold plate and had an unusual and yet familiar design on the crown – a signet ring of some sort.

"Wink, come here and take a shot of this ring, will you?"

"What? We going into the jewelry business?" he asked.

"No, but there's something awfully familiar about it. I want to check it out later." After he snapped a couple of pictures, the medics finished sealing up the body in the large bag and carried it downstairs and into the street on a stretcher.

"What do you make of it, Wink?" I asked as we made our way back into the smoke-filled hallway.

"Don't rightly know," he replied, snapping the plastic cover over the lens of his camera. "But I did hear two firemen talking and they thought the fire was started by that old guy smoking in bed. It'll be a day or two 'fore they'll say for sure."

Back in the street, firemen were rolling up hoses while police tried to keep the onlookers moving. The fire chief was still standing in the vicinity of the park talking with two homicide detectives. One of the cops was named Perkins, whom I didn't know very well. The other was Detective Phillip Mackey, a likable sort. One night when things were slow, I rode with Phil as he made the rounds on night shift. Short and skinny with a full head of wavy red hair, he reminded me a lot of the television detective Colombo. He had the coolest composure of any individual I knew. Very laid back. He could be boiling mad on the inside but not a ripple would show on the surface. The fireman had his back to me as I approached the trio and he continued talking to the detective once I was within earshot.

"The first man had already leaped from the fourth floor window up there by the time our first engine arrived. The other fellow jumped about two minutes later. Our people yelled for him to stop but he didn't hesitate. The halls were filled with smoke so we figure they panicked and decided to take their chances by jumping. Both were transported to the hospital where they were pronounced dead by the coroner."

"How about names, Chief? Have you identified them yet?" I interjected.

"You can get the details from my driver," he replied, spinning around to see who was asking the question. "The first man that jumped had identification on him. I think he was from Oklahoma. The other man we haven't identified yet."

"How about the guy that burned to death up there?"

"Haven't identified him yet either. The desk clerk said he thinks his name was Smith – probably an alias. They're checking it out now."

"I heard a rumor the fire started by somebody smoking in bed. Anything definite?" I asked.

"No," replied the white-haired fireman. "It's a possibility, but we don't have any evidence yet. How about just putting that the investigation is continuing for now, okay?" The inflection in his voice indicated that I was quickly wearing out my welcome.

As I turned around to look for Wink, I spotted Cris Carroll standing on a nearby curb, preparing to do a live interview with a witness to the blaze. Standing in the middle of the street and about eight feet away was a man focusing the mini-cam with the familiar WFLA-TV decal on it. Cris obviously got her cue from the nearby Channel 2 news truck for her facial expression suddenly came alive with a smile and flashing eyes. I have always envied television reporters their ability to change on at a moment's notice.

"Good morning. This is Cris Carroll with

a Channel 2 special report," she said, staring into the camera lens. "We're coming to you live this morning from in front of the historic Ashton Hotel in downtown Jacksonville where fire was discovered less than an hour ago. Three men are dead. Two of those victims died after they leaped from the building in an attempt to escape the flames. The other man was carried from the building only moments ago. We will have more details on the incident shortly."

The man standing next to Cris watched her with amazement, impressed with the way she handled herself and also terrified at being in front of a television camera.

"Standing with me is Milton Farber," Cris continued, turning a few degrees in the direction of the nervous man. "Mr. Farber is a visitor to our city and checked into the Ashton Hotel shortly before the fire was discovered. Tell us what you saw after checking in, Mr. Farber."

"Well, ma'am, after payin' the man at the front desk, I decided to go up to my room and get a little sleep. You see, I was on the road most of the night just gettin' here." Cris gave the man an impatient look in hopes he would spare her viewers the details. "Well, ma'am, the elevator wasn't working so I walked up the stairs. When I got up to about the third floor, that's when I smelled it. The smoke."

"What did you do then, Mr. Farber?"

"I hollered," he said with a toothless grin. "I ran back down the stairs but I hollered all the way. I tried to let them people know that the place was on fire."

"Thank you Mr. Farber," she said as she once again faced the camera. "Firemen are still trying to figure out exactly what happened here this morning. One report indicates the fire may have been started by a careless smoker.

"This has been a Channel 2 special report from the Ashton Hotel downtown. We will continue to keep you informed as more details become available. And now, back to you, John." That professional gaze drained from her face the minute she got the "off the air" signal. I walked over as she handed the microphone to one of the nearby technicians.

"Not bad," I said. "Getting better all the time."

"Thanks, Brad. The chief over there tell you anything more?"

"No, they probably won't know any details until this afternoon. How about some breakfast?"

"Sorry, I got to run. Rain check?"

"Anytime," I replied. After interviewing a couple of eyewitnesses and several tenants of the hotel, I went to the office and grabbed a sandwich in the employee cafeteria. Max was just finishing as I entered the dining room.

"How'd it go?"

"Okay," I replied. "I just wish these things would happen at a more decent hour."

"They never do," Max replied, munching on his tuna fish sandwich and reading over the morning's edition. "Wouldn't be news if they did."

"You know, Max, there was one thing I saw over there that appeared interesting. One of the men killed in the fire was wearing a ring with an unusual design. And it appeared to be gold-plated."

"What's so interesting about that?" he said.

"According to the desk clerk the guy had no money – a real indigent type. Slept down around the docks a lot. So doesn't it seem strange that a guy who couldn't afford a dinner half the time would be sporting a gold-plated ring?"

"Maybe so. But then maybe he lifted it off somebody."

"Yeah, I thought of that. But the thing that really intrigues me is that the design is similar to one that I saw in the stolen treasure last week." Max looked up from his paper, wiping his mouth with a paper napkin.

"You think it's part of the treasure?"

"I didn't say that. But it looked familiar. I couldn't be positive of anything. As soon as Wink develops the film, I'm going to take a picture over to that gal at the museum. Maybe she'll have some idea."

"By the way, how was your trip to Key West?" asked Max.

"All right. Nothing out of the ordinary."

"Did your friend Mr. Furman tell you he was in Tallahassee the night the treasure was stolen?"

"No-oo," I said, feeling sick in the pit of my stomach. There is nothing quite as sickening as being scooped on a story by your own boss. "How did you find out? What was he doing there?" Max gave me a smirky smile and took his time in doling out the information.

"One of the wire service guys over there was talking with some bureaucrat. Seems Furman was in town two weeks ago to confer with state officials on dividing up the treasure so he could sell his portion and raise money for his salvaging operation."

"Can anybody confirm that he was in Tallahassee that Sunday night?"

"Well, this offical that the correspondent talked to said he saw Furman at around 7 P.M., which doesn't mean anything. You know as well as I that he could have flown over here in a matter of minutes."

"When did he leave?"

"I understand he flew back to St. Petersburg early Monday morning," replied Max. "What did you learn in Key West?"

"As I said, very little. He has the two boats down there and appears to be running a rather simple salvaging operation. Lots of kids working for him. Everybody happy-go-lucky."

"Well, it could have just been coincidence. It just all seems a little fishy to me," he said.

After finishing my sandwich, I went upstairs and hammered out a story to go with Wink's photos of the fire:

THREE PERSONS DIE IN HOTEL FIRE

Two men leaped to their death and another died of massive burns following a three-alarm fire which swept through three floors of the Ashton Hotel Monday morning.

Officials identified the victims as Bernard Thompson, 42, of Tulsa, Oklahoma; William Wakeman, of Miami; and Isaac Smith, age and address unknown.

According to Fire Chief R.S. Batten, fire and rescue officials were called to the

Jacksonville hotel shortly after 8.30 A.M. Monday when smoke was observed in a wing on the fourth floor of the building.

The seven-story structure, which was constructed in 1912, is located at the corner of Market and Adams Streets, directly across from downtown Ashton Park.

Batten said most of the fire damage was limited to three rooms on the fourth floor of the building. He added that the hotel also suffered extensive smoke damage from the blaze.

Witnesses on their way to work told police that shortly after the alarm was sounded, Thompson appeared on a fourth floor window ledge and jumped without hesitation. He was taken to nearby Grady Memorial Hospital, where he was pronounced dead on arrival.

Shortly thereafter, Wakeman also crawled out onto a fourth floor ledge nearby and leaped to his death. It was later determined by the Duval County medical examiner that Wakeman apparently died of a broken neck he suffered in the fall.

"The first man jumped before our people arrived," said Batten. "Shortly after they got here, Wakeman also climbed out and jumped, even though our men yelled for him to stop."

Batten said he believes the two were asleep when the blaze occurred and were probably

95

startled by the sudden noise of the fire engines and people yelling.

"The fourth floor hallways were filled with smoke by the time we got up there," he said. "I don't think they (the victims) thought there was any other way out."

The third victim of the fire, Smith, was discovered by firemen in his fourth floor room with third-degree burns over 90 percent of his body. He was also taken to Grady Hospital where he was pronounced dead.

"The room in which we discovered the victim was very close to where the fire originated," he said.

Batten added that an investigation into the cause of the fire is continuing, although one official commented that the blaze may have been started by a careless smoker.

According to John Wren, one of the owners of the building, officials of the city's fire department had inspected the hotel within the last few months and had determined that fire hazard violations in the 75-year-old structure were minimal. Firemen at the scene refused to comment.

One man who had been a resident of the building for the past four months, said that all three victims of the fire had only rented rooms recently.

"You get to know the faces of the old

timers," he said. "They was (sic) all pretty new there. Ike (Smith) has been around town for some time. But he had only been staying at the hotel a week or so.

The man added that Smith was a heavy smoker and could possibly have started the fire by smoking in bed.

Batten estimated damage to the building and contents at $100,000.

One of the last remaining buildings of the turn-of-the-century period, the Ashton had suffered a decline in business over recent years. Wren refused to comment as to whether the damage to the hotel would be repaired.

The hotel was named in honor of Senator Philip Ashton, one of the first representatives from Florida to serve in Washington after the peninsula was declared a state in 1845.

After making a few corrections on the copy and gluing the takes together with rubber cement, I dropped the story off at the city desk and stopped by the photo department on the way out.

"How did the photos of the ring come out, Wink?"

"Not bad under the conditions, I guess. At least you can make out the design. That's what you wanted, right?" he said, handing me the black and white photos from the print dryer.

"Yeah, this is great," I replied. "Thanks."

It was mid-afternoon by the time I got over to the museum. Gail Tomlinson was talking on the phone with a gallery in New York when I arrived.

"Hello, Mr. Norris," she said, putting down the receiver. "Have you any good news concerning the treasure?"

"Perhaps," I said. "Does this look familiar?" I asked, handing her the photographs of the ring that Wink had taken in the burned-out hotel room. Her face tightened up a bit as she stared at the pictures.

"Wh-why yes, where did you get these?"

"A man who burned to death in a hotel fire this morning was wearing that ring when they found him. Can you tell me for sure whether that was part of the treasure?" I asked.

"Well, no, I can't be positive. But there was a ring in the collection that looked just like this. If the ring in this picture isn't from the collection, then it is an awfully good copy," she replied, still studying the photographs.

"I don't think it was a copy. I think somebody has found at least part of that treasure. The trouble is how come an old bum who gets burned to death in a flophouse turns out to be the number one suspect?"

"That, I guess," said the young woman, "is for the police to find out."

"Yes, I suppose so. By the way, did you know that Furman was in Tallahassee the night the jewels were stolen?"

Gail's eyes got wide at the mention of his name but she regained her composure quickly. "Furman?"

"Adolf Furman. He's the man that owns the company that discovered the treasure."

"No, I didn't know he was in Tallahassee. Should I?"

"I guess not," I said. "I just figured he might have called you or something."

"I've never met this Mr. Furman. I believe I did talk to him on the phone once after the robbery took place. But I've never met the man. The treasure was being handled by a public relations firm out of Miami and they're the only people I've talked to about the jewels."

"That's too bad," I said, shifting my weight as I stood in front of her large desk. "I flew down to Key West over the weekend and got to see his operation. You would find it very interesting, the way they look for the buried treasure and all."

"I'm sure it's interesting," she said, trying to be pleasant.

"Which reminds me. While I was out on his ship, I ran into a girl that claims she knows you."

"Yes?" Gail Tomlinson watched me intently, wondering what name I would drop on her.

"Her name was Candy. I'm afraid I didn't catch her last name. A rather tall girl with long hair – a brunette."

"I'm sorry, Mr. Norris, but I only know a few Candys and none of them live in the Keys."

"But this girl said she was a student at Florida Atlantic University."

"No, I don't know any Candys there either. She must have gotten me mixed up with somebody else."

"I suppose so," I said. "Tell me, Gail. Are you married?"

"What's that got to do with any of this?" she demanded.

"Well, nothing really. I'm single and I thought if you were too, maybe you'd like to go out for dinner sometime."

"I'm sorry," she said, some of the anxiety draining from her face. "This whole business has been awfully hard to take. The job here as director is the first and only job I've had since graduating from college. And nothing like this has ever happened before, I can assure

100

you. Yes, I'm single and dinner sounds good sometime." Her dark blue pantsuit complimented her blond hair. I could tell from the two times that I had met her that she spent a lot of money on clothes.

"Great," I said. "Besides, you shouldn't get too upset about any of this anyway. As far as I'm concerned, it's just another good story. Why don't we make it Friday night? That's one of my nights off."

"Sounds fine to me," she said. "But you'll have to pick me up after 8:30 P.M. because we don't close here until seven."

"See you then," I replied. "Where do you live?"

"The Sand Flea Apartments over on Post Street," she replied. "Number 36."

"Hey, isn't that where the Johnson girl lived?"

"Yes," Gail said, looking rather irritated that I had brought the subject up again. "She rented an apartment there but I didn't know her at all. I mean, I had spoken to her coming and going a couple of times. But never to actually talk, you know? It was just one of those things."

"Did the police come and talk to you about it?"

"Oh yes," she replied. "They were here a day or two after the robbery and asked questions for a couple of hours. But there just wasn't anything to tell. Nothing but pure coincidence. After all, it does have a reputation as being a good singles complex, you know?"

"Yeah, I've heard that." As a matter of fact, I had chased after a beautiful redhead with long legs who had lived there until a few months before. I remember sitting by the swimming pool and thinking what a haven for beautiful women the place was.

"Hey, I'd better be going," I said, turning to go. "See you Friday night."

"Right. Friday night."

It was a little before 3:30 P.M. by the time I made it over to the medical examiner's office adjoining Grady Hospital. Dr. Samuel Lin, head of the department, was bent over a cadaver as I walked through the double doors of the outer lobby and into the laboratory. Standing next to Lin was Lieutenant Marler, obviously as interested in the dead man as I was.

"Hello, Doc. Finished with the autopsy on those three guys from this morning's fire?" Marler flashed a scowl of disgust, clearly indicating his displeasure at my presence in an area over which he had no jurisdiction to order me out.

"Hello, Brad," replied Dr. Lin, not

bothering to look up. "We should be through soon."

Lin was examining the body of Smith while I assumed the two shapes beneath white sheets on carts against the back wall were the bodies of the two men who had jumped from the hotel windows earlier.

Dr. Lin had been the Duval County Medical Examiner for almost fifteen years and was liked by all who knew him. Of Oriental descent, Lin's parents had moved to San Francisco before he was born. After attending the University of California Medical School, Lin practiced forensic medicine in Los Angeles before accepting the Jacksonville job.

A man of medium height and a soft voice, he could always be found with a pair of black hornrimmed glasses balanced perfectly on the bridge of his nose. He was tops when it came to solving homicide. The number of cases he had cracked when detectives could discover no clues were too numerable to count.

As I walked up to the examining table, a rush of nausea was suddenly replaced with simple curiosity. People often ask me how I can cover bad traffic accidents and I try to explain that you're so busy trying to get the story that you don't have time to even think about getting sick until well after the story has been filed.

"Have you found anything more on our Mr. Smith here, Lieutenant?"

"Naw, nothing yet. Looks like he was smoking in bed and fell asleep. You know, the usual."

"Where's the ring, Doc?"

"Over on the table with the rest of his possessions," Lin replied, pointing toward a white porcelain table with the scalpel he was holding in his hand. I walked over and held the ring up to the light for a closer inspection.

"So he picked up a dime store ring someplace. Big deal," said Marler from behind me.

"Nice snow job, Lieutenant," I said. "But I've known you long enough to know that you've done your homework and are aware that this ring is in fact part of the collection the Johnson woman took off the bridge with her a week ago."

"We know nothing of the kind," he added, a hint of anger in his voice over the fact that I had stumbled onto the connection. "It may look like the ring but we have nothing positive yet."

"How about Gail Tomlinson for starters," I added. "I had Wink take a couple of pictures of the ring at the hotel this morning and the girl over at the museum positively identified the ring as part of the collection."

"You gonna print that?"

"I'm going to say that the ring found on Smith's body closely resembled one taken in the collection from the museum. I realize it makes your people look bad, but I can't sit on this stuff. The television stations would sure run it if they had it and I can't take the chance on them accidentally finding out. Max would fire me if I sat on the story and got scooped, you know that."

"Okay, how about saying the police discovered the connection. And you can add to it that Smith is believed to have been in the vicinity of the bridge on the night the girl jumped with the treasure."

"Oh, yeah?" I asked, taking a notepad from my shirt pocket. I put the ring back on the table and Marler turned to walk back over to the examining table. "Where exactly in the vicinity of the bridge?"

"We understand he used to sleep under the concrete bridge supports when he was down on cash. A couple of his drinking friends near the docks said he hadn't had any work in almost a month but shortly after the robbery he took a room at the Ashton."

"Any idea where his windfall came from?" I asked.

"Nope. We figured he might have found some more of the treasure and hocked it in one of the local pawnshops. Our men are checking it out now."

Lin was continuing his investigation of the victim's body. In addition to most of his upper torso and the lower part of one leg, much of Smith's face had been badly burned in the fire.

"I don't think we are going to find much more from our examination, gentlemen," Lin exclaimed. "Mr. Smith here obviously died from massive burns and from smoke inhalation. Based on the burn patterns on his right hand and clothes, and also the presence of nicotine burned into the flesh. I would say it's safe to assume the victim was smoking at the time of the fire."

"Well, I guess that settles it," Marler said. "Too bad he died. I would have liked to have asked him a few questions about how he got that ring."

"Fate is not often cooperative, Lieutenant," Lin said in a soft voice. Marler just shrugged his shoulders.

"So that rules out any foul play, right Doc?" I asked.

"We'll not have the final lab reports until

morning," he replied. "But I would say that it is safe to assume at this point that there was no foul play involved."

"Which leaves the unanswered question of where is the rest of the treasure, and especially the diamond necklace."

"Still at the bottom of the river more than likely," added Marler. "That ring probably just washed up on the bank and Smith happened to find it among the rocks."

"I don't buy it Lieutenant," I said. "Maybe in the ocean where you have strong tides, but not in the middle of a river. No ring is going to wash thirty-five feet up from the bottom."

"So what's your theory? You think this old derelict here swam to the bottom and helped himself to the jewels?" The policeman gestured toward the body and I had to smile a bit. It was amazing to me how easy it was to ruffle his feathers. I guess it came from his many years of having to deal with the press. God, how it must wear down even the best of men.

"I don't have the answers either. Let's just hope we get lucky and find some more jewels on some more people in a little better condition than Mr. Smith here."

Dr. Lin had once again covered the victim's body with a sheet and was filling out some forms at a desk in a corner of the room.

"I should have the results of the autopsy ready by mid-morning tomorrow, Lieutenant," he said. "You can send one of your men to pick it up around eleven."

"Thanks, Doc, I'll do that." The phone rang as we walked toward the door. It was for Marler. For about two minutes, he listened to the voice on the other end of the phone and then put down the receiver.

"Well, Norris, we may have run into a little of that luck you were talking about," he said. "That was my office. It seems a city employee found a bag under the bridge that may be tied to the robbery."

"Well, what are we waiting for?"

"We?"

"Give me a front page story and I'll get you elected sheriff," I said, gently pushing him out the door. "Think of it – your own plush office, a limousine, nice hours . . ."

7

Marler's green '76 Dodge Dart kicked up a cloud of dust as we drove down the narrow dirt service road toward the bridge supports located on the western bank of the river. A man dressed in white shirt and gray slacks was talking with two plainclothes detectives as we pulled up and parked next to their white sedan with the yellow city license plate.

"Lieutenant, this is Stuart Eisenberg, the guy that found the bag," mumbled one of the detectives, his .38-caliber revolver bulging from beneath his J.C. Penney sports coat.

Marler took the bag from the other detective and began spinning it in his hand, examining it from every angle. It was a rectangular plastic money bag with a zipper at the top – the type of bag that banks give to their customers for making deposits. Embossed on the side was the emblem of the Mediterranean Maritime Company.

"How about prints?" Marler asked.

"None except Eisenberg's. Nothing inside either, except this coin." The policeman took a rather dull doubloon from his coat pocket and handed it to Marler.

"Did you find anything in the bag other than this coin, Mr. Eisenberg?" Marler's gaze shifted from the coin in his hand to the stranger's eyes in an attempt to lock him in a stare.

"No, only that," Eisenberg replied, careful not to return the gaze. "The bag was over there in a clump of grass near that piling when I found it."

"What were you doing back here, anyway?"

"I work for the State Department of Engineers and Inspection. We're responsible for inspecting these bridges on a routine basis for any structural wear and damage."

Eisenberg was a man of medium height with a slight paunch to his otherwise thin frame. He appeared to be in his mid-40s with a bushy black mustache that perfectly matched his coarse jet black hair. As Marler continued to study the bag and the surrounding area, the state inspector shuffled from one foot to the other in anticipation of the lieutenant's next question.

"You guys come down here often?"

"Not from the inspection department," Eisenberg said. "I was down here about three months ago but not since. I've been up on the bridge a couple of times but not down here."

Marler walked over to a dusty spot of ground where the bag had supposedly been discovered. Next to the spot, a piling about six feet square rose about thirty-five feet into the air where it helped to support the massive bridge. From the ground, the overall size of the bridge was awesome.

"Right here, Lieutenant. It was right about here that I found the bag. I remembered reading something about the robbery and all last week. So when I looked inside and saw the coin, I figured it might be important. That's when I called your people."

The homicide inspector turned to one of the detectives standing behind him.

"Have you checked this area clean?"

"Yes, sir. We made a general check of the area and found nothing. However, we did find bits of an old bedroll and some junk up in that crawlspace over there – could be where that old man used to do his camping."

"Ike Smith?" Marler asked, somewhat pleased at the thought that there might be a tie-in to the whole confusing mess.

"Just a hunch," the detective replied. "I called for a couple of ET boys to come over and have a look."

Fifty feet away, the pilings rose fifteen feet above the ground and ran up to meet the asphalt incline where the bridge began. Above the earth and cement and beneath the steel girders was an area that looked diminutive from a distance yet appeared large enough up close for a man to crawl into.

"Brad Norris, *Chronicle*," I said, extending my hand. "You familiar with the case of the woman jumping here last week?" Eisenberg stared at me with that unblinking gaze I see so often. It's the look of initial fear when the little guy on the street first encounters a newspaper reporter about to smear his name

111

all over the front page of tomorrow's edition.

"Uh, yeah. I remember reading about it. Do you think this is connected?"

"Well, it looks that way. The girl that jumped worked for the same company where that bag came from. And there were some coins stolen from the museum similar to the one you found in the bag."

"Have they found any sign of the body?"

"Not yet," I replied. "I understand they found a piece of clothing near here that matched a description of the clothes she was wearing when she jumped. But no sign of the body as yet."

Eisenberg took a pipe from the pocket of his jacket and began tamping tobacco into the bowl with a small silver instrument. "Well, if that's part of the treasure, then I wonder where the rest of it is. I guess this makes me the prime suspect."

"Not exactly," I said. "In that hotel fire this morning, a man who burned to death was wearing a gold ring that also appears to have been part of the stolen collection. Some of his friends said he used to sleep around here so he might have stumbled across it."

Two police evidence technicians had unloaded their equipment from the panel truck and had followed Marler and the others over to the steel bridge supports. Puffing his pipe, Marler stood on the west bank of the river staring across the water toward the far side.

"Are they still looking for the woman, Mr. Norris?" he asked over his shoulder, not bothering to turn around.

"Uh, yeah, I guess so."

"Probably won't find her, you know. Body has no doubt washed out to sea by now."

"They might not, but I doubt the body could have traveled that far," I said. "This river meanders for 20 miles before it opens to the Atlantic. That's a long way for a body to travel without being noticed."

"Yes, it is. But look at those whirlpools out there in the middle of the river. I'd say that current is moving at better than ten knots. Water moving that fast could carry an object like a body a long distance unless it snagged on something."

The Andover Bridge must be observed from beneath to truly appreciate its size. The mammoth columns of concrete and steel rise almost three hundred feet in the air. Completed in 1955 at a cost of almost $12 million, the bridge provides one of the finest examples of engineering in the entire southeast.

"Is there a special name for this kind of a bridge?" I asked.

"Yes, it's called a three-span cantilever bridge," Eisenberg replied, pointing to the concrete buttresses protruding from the water. "They call it that because most of the bridge's weight is balanced on those two main supports out there."

"Hmm. What's the advantage?"

"Well, it's ideal for this location because it eliminates the need for a center support. And since this is a port city, the tankers can pass easily beneath because there's almost a thousand feet of space between those two center supports."

The cars passing overhead looked like toys and could barely be heard from where we were standing.

"How much clearance is there between the water level and the bottom of the bridge, anyway?" I asked.

"Vertical clearance is 149 feet," he replied matter-of-factly. "The eastern approach to the bridge is 3,447 feet long while the western approach to the bridge is 2,306 feet. The central span connecting the two is 810 feet long, so I guess you could say that the total length of the bridge is about 6,500 feet in length."

"Whew. Is there anything about this bridge you don't know?"

Eisenberg gave a faint smile, obviously

proud of his knowledge concerning the bridge's vital statistics. "When I moved here twenty-five years ago, I was fresh out of engineering school and looking for work. I was eventually hired by the city's planning department and assigned to the Andover Bridge Project which had just moved out of the design stages and begun construction. For the next two and a half years, I lived this bridge. Knew every nut and bolt. Stood on this very spot and watched as they poured ton after ton of cement and concrete into place. I doubt if there is anybody alive that knows this bridge as well as I do."

"How deep would you say the channel is right here?" I asked.

"About forty or fifty feet, I'd say."

"Really?" I exclaimed. "I would have thought it only about half that."

Eisenberg walked to a point on the bank where the river elbowed and pointed toward the Acosta Bridge which spanned the river about a mile to the west.

"South of that bridge, the river is about half a mile wide. Then it narrows at the bridge to about six hundred feet across. Couple with that the fact that the river suddenly elbows to the right about forty-five degrees. When you force that much water through a narrow opening and twist it to boot, you speed up the flow." As he continued to talk, the engineer pointed to the portion of water directly in front of us. "Same thing happens here. It widens a bit east of the Acosta Bridge but by the time it reaches this point, you have another bend in the river and it narrows again. That's what causes those whirlpools. The water strikes that far bank and just starts spinning."

"Which still leaves the big question of what happened to the woman's body," I added.

Small wisps of pipe smoke curled from between Eisenberg's lips and through his mustache as he continued to gaze at the water's edge.

"Since you haven't spotted the body yet and it has been over a week, I'd say it's safe to assume the body has snagged on something," he said. "If the victim goes under and swallows a lot of water, they'll usually sink. But as the body decomposes internally, it creates a gas which should cause the body to rise to the surface."

"And how long should that normally take?"

"Normally, anywhere from twenty-four to seventy-two hours."

"So you think the body has gotten hooked on something down there, right?"

"It's very possible," he answered. "When they build a bridge, anything that isn't needed

116

goes into the water. Pilings, concrete, scraps. Since ships use the channel, they would normally not clutter it up. But the river is so deep and the current so swift here, it would take a lot to fill it up. Consequently, the fairly sandy bottom looks like a junkyard down there."

Marler and his entourage of detectives and technicians made their way back from the cement culvert. The evidence men returned to their truck and began securing their equipment.

"Thanks for your help," Marler told Eisenberg. "Our men have a phone number and will get in touch if we need any more information."

"What did you find in that crawlspace, Lieutenant?" I asked. "Anything that would tie Ike Smith to it?"

"Lot of junk mostly," he replied. "We took a few samples which we'll give to Lin and see if he can match." Marler took the coin from his pocket and handed it to me. "Does this look like one of the pieces from the museum theft?" It appeared to be an authentic doubloon in fairly good condition. On one side was printed the familiar insignia of the 17th century Spanish crown while several designs and markings were engraved on the opposite side.

"I dunno. There were some coins like this that were taken in the heist," I said. "And this doubloon does look like the real thing. But there are a lot of these things floating around. Whether you can positively identify this as part of the *Augustin* treasure, I just don't know."

"Wonder how much it's worth."

"Probably not all that much," I said, handing back the coin. "Any local dealer could tell you easy enough. He might be able to tell you a little more about where it came from, too."

Marler gave the coin to a detective, who in turn handed it over to one of the evidence technicians.

"Even if we tie this whole thing in, the woman jumped from the middle of the bridge. How could the bag have gotten all the way over here on shore?" the detective asked.

"Maybe she threw it," I replied.

"A quarter of a mile?"

"Well, that's no more far-fetched than the idea that she swam over here, took the jewels out of the bag and ran away."

"You're right there. None of this makes sense," Marler said. "We're pretty sure there weren't any small boats down here that night. And besides, why toss the bag here, leaving behind the evidence?"

"Right again, Lieutenant," I said. "The only person who would have left the bag here would have been somebody who didn't care whether it was found or not. And that description fits Mr. Smith."

"Yeah, I hope some of that junk can be traced back to him. I'd sure like to wrap up this screwy case."

Traffic on the Andover Bridge above us was beginning to thicken as office workers crowded each other in an effort to escape the inner city rush and get to the suburbs and their long-awaited cocktails. The honking horns and racing engines reminded me that I'd have to hurry in order to get back to the newsroom and write a couple of takes in time for the first edition.

8

Leaving Jacksonville before dawn, I arrived on the campus of St. Petersburg University by noon. Located on twenty acres of land bordering Tampa Bay, it's a pretty place with neatly manicured lawns and buildings designed in the Spanish manner.

After parking my Mustang in the visitors'

area of the parking lot, I wandered around until I found the building containing the registrar's office. A middle-aged woman with black hair and bi-focal glasses balanced on the tip of her nose looked up from her reading as I walked through the door.

"Good afternoon," she said in a routine manner. "May I help you?"

"Yes, thank you," I said, walking up to the waist-high formica counter that separated us. "My name is Brad Norris and I write for the Jacksonville *Chronicle*. I'm trying to locate a young woman who I understand attended this university a couple of years ago."

"Well, let's see," she said, getting up from her desk. "What is the young woman's name?"

"Vicki Johnson."

"And when did she graduate?"

"I don't believe she graduated."

"I see. Do you know when exactly she was enrolled here?"

"Not exactly," I replied. "But it would have been about three years ago – maybe four."

"Getting that information may take a little time," the woman replied. "We don't keep the records on undergraduates readily available. If you like to have a seat or perhaps come back, I should be able to have the information you need in about a half hour."

"Thank you," I said. "I believe I'll have a look around your campus in the meantime. Where might I find the library?"

"Just go out the door at the end of this hallway," she said, "and it is the first building to your left. You can't miss it."

There were few students about; there rarely are many during summer term. The air felt good as it blew in from the bay and across the campus. But the hot sun made it too uncomfortable to stay outside so I ran for the air-conditioning in the library. While waiting there, I thought about looking in the old college yearbooks to see if I could find Vicki Johnson's picture. My idea paid off. Her photograph was included in the freshman class section of the 1976 yearbook. It was a little strange staring at the face of the woman who had jumped off the bridge. It was the first picture I had seen of her and I had conjured up a totally different image in my mind. It's kind of like seeing a radio disc jockey for the first time after you have listened to him for some time and tried to imagine what he looked like by the sound of his voice. Vicki Johnson had a thin face and deep-set eyes. And her hair was cut short in a page-boy style. I had pictured someone a little

121

softer looking although I didn't know why.

In the back of the yearbook, it listed her address as Venice, Florida. There were no extra-curricular activities listed under her name.

I leafed through an old issue of *Newsweek* in order to kill remaining time. After about twenty minutes, I wandered back to the administration building and the black-haired woman who was helping me. She smiled as I walked through the glass door, indicating she had been successful in locating the information I wanted.

"I believe I have located the woman you were looking for," she said, peeling open a stack of computerized print-out sheets. "We had a Vicki Johnson enrolled as a freshman in 1976. Does that sound like the right person?"

"That's the one," I said. "I saw her picture in the yearbook over at the library."

"I'm afraid that is about all I can tell you about her. According to these records, she dropped out sometime after the first semester of her sophomore year."

"What about her parents? The yearbook listed her address as Venice, Florida."

"Yes, this shows her address as Venice, too. But I don't know whether it's still accurate. I don't have a father's name here, only a woman's. Doris Johnson of 1412 Sunrise Boulevard."

"Is there anybody on campus that might have known Vicki?" I asked. "You know, that might still remember her?"

"That I couldn't tell you," the woman behind the counter said. "Since she was an undergraduate, she wouldn't have had a counselor, at least not a personal one. But judging from this printout, she did take several athletic courses while she was here. Rowing, sailing, swimming – those would have been under Miss Pembroke, our women's athletic director. And she was here in 1976, the same time as your Miss Johnson. You might ask her if you like. She might remember something."

"Thanks again for all your help," I said, jotting down a few notes in my memo-book on the way out the door. A check with the Venice information turned up negative. There was no phone listed to a Doris Johnson.

I was told at the gym that Nancy Pembroke was out on the bay in a sailboat teaching students how to maneuver the craft without turning it over. Sitting on the bank, I could make out the billowing sail about a mile and a half away. I knew it had to be her since the emblem of the university was emblazoned on the sail. A nearby student said they were

123

due in soon so I decided to make myself comfortable on the pier and enjoy the view. I didn't have to wait long.

"You must be Nancy Pembroke," I said after they had tied up the boat and the young students had taken off for the nearest soft-drink machine. "I'm Brad Norris and I work for the newspaper in Jacksonville."

"Hello. You're a long way from home, aren't you?"

"Yes. I'm trying to get a little information about a girl who took some courses under you a couple of years ago. Her name was Vicki Johnson. Do you remember her?"

"Vaguely," she replied. "What did you want to know?"

"Anything you can remember about her."

"Well, I'd like to help you, Mr. Norris, but there are a lot of students that go through here. I remember the name but I'm afraid that is about it. Can't you talk to her and get what you need?"

"That's the trouble. We think she's dead."

"Dead?"

"A couple of weeks ago, she apparently jumped off a bridge in Jacksonville with more than a million dollars in Spanish treasure. The police haven't been able to come up with anything – no sign of her or the treasure."

"I remember reading something about that

124

in the local paper," she said. "But I didn't place the name." Miss Pembroke laid some life preservers and nylon rope she had been carrying on the grass. Then she turned and faced me once again. "I'm afraid I still can't help you. I think she left here about three years ago. But I can barely remember what she looked like."

"If you can spare a minute, would you walk with me over to the library and look at her picture in the yearbook? Maybe the face will help jog your memory a little."

Miss Pembroke walked with me to the library where she looked at Vicki Johnson's picture. "Yes, I remember her now. But I still don't think I can tell you a lot. There was nothing unusual about her. Your standard 18-year-old girl with all the typical hang-ups, goals and frustrations of a young woman her age."

"The woman in the registrar's office said she took a lot of your courses like sailing and rowing."

"She seemed to enjoy the water a lot. Signed up for anything that was on or near the water. But then, most of these kids do. I think it comes from growing up around the water."

"What kind of a swimmer was she?"

"Very good – a strong swimmer," the

woman said. "Vicki was on the university swim team her first year here. She wasn't that fast but she was strong. She could go the distance."

"Did she have any close friends you can remember?"

"No, not that I can remember. She seemed to get along well with the others in her class. Taking a sailing course isn't exactly like studying calculus. It takes teamwork, learning to run the boat as one solid unit. And she was a good team member. Got along well with the others in her class."

"Thanks for your time," I said, walking with the woman instructor out the front door of the library. I realized I wasn't going to get any more useful information out of her. "If you can think of anything else about Vicki that might be helpful, would you give me a call in Jacksonville? Call collect."

"Sure," she said, taking my business card. I had turned and taken about ten steps toward the parking lot when she called after me.

"You know, Mr. Norris, now that I think about it, I believe Vicki had a relative living here in St. Pete. A half-sister or something."

"Really? Do you remember her name?"

"I'm trying to think. Vicki told me about her once. The reason I remember is because she was a stripper or something like that.

Vicki was upset about it because it had created some family problems."

"Do you remember where she was working?"

"A place over on Maderia Beach called Frankie's as I remember. Can't miss the place – it's right on the main drag. I think the girl's name was Bridgette – at least, that's the name she went by. I'm sure she's long gone by now."

"I'll check it out," I said as I turned to leave. "You've been a big help."

Nancy Pembroke was right. A large plastic sign about twenty feet off the ground announced the location of Frankie's Lounge and Package Store. The parking lot was empty save for a few cars parked near the side of the building. It was a medium-sized building, all covered with those wooden shingles to give the place a rustic effect. The inside of the bar was very dark and had the damp smell of a room where the air-conditioning had been turned off for some time. The dampness was mixed with the smell of stale beer.

Taking a stool near the corner, I ordered a draught beer and watched a girl dancing on the stage behind the bar. She was bumping and grinding to a Bee Gees record that blared out of the speakers suspended from the ceiling. By the time I walked in, she had already stripped down to a revealing bra and pair of black lace panties. Two guys sitting at a table in the back were whistling and clapping for her to speed up the process. She smiled and wiggled her large breasts in their direction. Ah, for the love of an audience.

The pretty young thing danced through two more songs before stripping all the way down to a small, sequined G-string. She was a very good dancer. Each thrust of her pelvis was timed exactly with the beat of the song coming from the speakers. Her legs were long and slender and her buttocks rounded and not too large. Her stomach was trim and completely devoid of the stretch marks which seem to be a trademark of the striptease business. But perhaps the most intriguing thing about her was her sexy smile. She was not what you would call beautiful. Yet she had the coy smile of a person for whom you would do almost anything to sleep with. I found myself getting excited.

The music stopped and the girl with the beautiful body disappeared behind the curtain after blowing a kiss to the two guys at the back table. While waiting for the next act to begin, I motioned the bartender for another beer.

"I'm looking for a dancer by the name of Bridgette," I said as he placed the cold

128

draught in front of me. "Is there anybody here by that name?"

"You just saw her buddy."

"Yeah? I would like to talk to her if that's possible. Would you tell her I'd like to buy her a beer."

"Bridgette happens to like champagne," the bartender said.

"Fine," I said, holding back the smile. It reminded me of a story I did on places like that a couple of months before. The horny patrons buy the girls what they think is expensive champagne but what is really Seven-Up in a fancy glass. The girls then split the cost of the drink with the house and pocket the money. It's an old scam but I figured it was worth the money to get the information I wanted.

A familiar Rolling Stones song suddenly filled the bar and a short and somewhat pudgy girl dressed in a white feather costume danced onto the stage. She looked pleasant but was obviously not the featured attraction. The guys sitting at the table in the back didn't seem to mind, though. They clapped and whistled just as loud for the feather dancer as they had for Bridgette.

"Hello, my name is Bridgette," the young girl said as she slipped into the barstool next to mine.

"Hi. Brad Norris," I said, shaking her hand. "I must say you have a beautiful body."

"Thanks." The bartender brought her the soda in a champagne glass and I put a five on the counter to cover my tab.

"Why don't we sit at one of those tables in the back so we can talk," I said.

"Fine," she said. "But I'll tell you right up front. I don't go home with you and I don't give hand jobs under the table."

"Right," I said, the thought never having occurred to me until she had mentioned it.

"What'd you say your name was?" she asked.

"Brad. Brad Norris. I write for the Jacksonville *Chronicle* newspaper."

"I should have known," she said with a smirk. "And you want to interview me to see how I like being a stripper. When I first saw you, I didn't think you looked like a guy on the make. But you don't look hard enough to be a cop. I shoulda figured you out."

"I'm not here to do a story about strippers," I said. "I'm looking into the death of a girl I understand you were related to."

"Vicki?" she asked.

"Yes. Was she your sister?"

"Cousin. But I grew up with her mother and her, so I guess you could say we were

130

kinda sisters. I still can't believe she could have done what they say she did."

"Well, they haven't been able to find her or the treasure she supposedly took. That's why I'm down here."

"You're wasting your time here," the young woman said. "I haven't seen Vicki for more than a year. Haven't talked to her either. The only word I've gotten was a letter from her a couple of months back."

"What did she have to say?"

"The usual. Wanted to know how I was doing – the whole bit," she said, lighting up a Marlboro. "Said she was working for some shipping company and liked it okay."

"Vicki's mother lives in Venice?" I asked.

"Used to. She moved in with a sister in Miami about a year ago. I haven't heard from her, either. But then we haven't talked since I started dancing here about three years ago."

"Did Vicki used to come over here when she went to the university?"

"Hell no," Bridgette said with a chuckle. "When I started dancing here, Vicki's mama started raising all kinds of hell. Said I was goin' to the devil – you know, all that fire and brimstone crap. Well, Vicki tried to patch things up between me and her mama. But it was no use and she stopped comin' around after a while."

"She tried to get you to stop?"

"Yeah, right. But I was datin' Frankie at the time, you know, and I wasn't about to leave. Me and Frankie are just friends now but I stayed anyway. The money is okay and I get to spend the days on the beach." I couldn't help noticing how nice her breasts looked beneath the sheer black top she was wearing. The bra she had on exposed all but the nipples. Modesty prevented me from staring but I sneaked a glance whenever she looked away.

"Tell me, Bridgette, did Vicki have any other friends around here that you knew of?"

"My real name is Beverly but you can call me Bev. All my friends do," she said. "I think Vicki kept pretty much to herself. There were a couple of kids over at that school that hung around together. But I don't think they were very close. I don't think Vicki kept up with any of them after she left."

"When Vicki wrote to you, did she mention anything about the treasure or money problems? Anything that might be tied in to all of this?"

"Nothing," Bev said, blowing a smoke ring across the small wooden table. I glanced over her shoulder at the pudgy girl on the stage who was now down to her G-string and

132 ·

humping in the direction of the bartender's head. "Vicki mostly talked about family stuff. Mentioned how her mama was doin' and said she'd been seeing some guy up in Jacksonville. That's about it."

"Did she mention the guy's name?" I asked.

"No, I don't think so. I'm afraid I didn't keep the letter. But he was some kind of a professional man as I remember. She mentioned what he did for a living but I forget now. Maybe a doctor or something. I dunno what."

A waitress came over to our table and offered to bring more drinks but I declined.

"I still find it all pretty hard to believe," Bev said. "Vicki was really down to earth. She didn't do things like that. Now me, that's different. But I can't picture Vicki takin' so much as a piece of candy, let alone that treasure they said she took. She must have been in some kind of trouble. Or maybe she got to runnin' with the wrong people."

"Thanks for your help," I said. "I've got to be going."

"Good luck," she replied as she slid out from behind the booth. "I hope you find out what really happened to Vicki. We weren't very close but she was a nice kid. It always happens to the nice ones, you know?"

"Yes, I know."

Before leaving the lounge, I got the address of Furman's St. Pete office out of the phone book. The building turned out to be a small, one-story concrete block building on a side street about four blocks from the municipal pier. There was a small, hand-painted wooden sign over the door which read OFF SHORE DIVERS, INC. I parked the Mustang in the stone driveway beside the building and went inside. The only person in the office was a rather plump, aged woman with red hair and a mole on her right cheek.

"Hi," I said, closing the door quickly to keep the hot air outside. "I'm looking for Mr. Furman. Is he around?"

"No, I'm afraid he's in Key West at the moment. Is there anything I could help you with?"

"Not really," I replied. "My name is Brad Norris and I'm a reporter with the Jacksonville *Chronicle*. I met Mr. Furman in Key West last week and I was in the area so I thought I'd drop in."

"He'll be sorry he missed you, I'm sure. I'm afraid he won't be back until the week after next at the earliest."

"Will you tell him I stopped by to say hello?"

"I'll do that," she said. "You say you're

134

from Jacksonville? Have they found anything new on the treasure that was stolen?"

"As a matter of fact, they have." The woman's eyes perked up. "They found a money bag under the bridge with a doubloon inside. No sign of the rest of the treasure yet but they're still looking."

"At least that's something!" she said with a smile. "Maybe they'll get lucky and find the rest of it."

I turned as if to leave but stopped once I reached the door.

"Oh, I almost forgot. There was a woman who attended the university here. A woman by the name of Vicki Johnson. Did she ever work for Mr. Furman that you can remember?"

"Vicki Johnson ... Johnson," the woman with the mole said as she contemplated the name. "No, never heard that name before." She had quite a poker face and I questioned her sincerity. Maybe she had that blank expression all the time.

"Are you sure? Maybe if you checked your records."

"No need for that," she replied. "Never forget a name. And I know for sure, never had a woman named Vicki Johnson working here before."

"Fine. Give Mr. Furman my regards." As

135

I walked toward the car, I noticed a small, fenced-in area behind the office. The gate was closed but unlocked. I could make out several rows of shelves behind the fence, containing what looked like marine equipment. Opening the gate and walking into the yard, I picked up a couple of metal canisters and examined them more closely. Most of the equipment looked like it had been used, evidently a parts warehouse for Furman's two salvage boats.

I didn't hear any footsteps behind me. But I did see the blur of motion as it swung toward my head. I saw it just in time to move a few inches and avoid the direct force of a blow. My assailant was a husky man with large, muscular arms and a denim cap pulled over his head. His large fist caught me on the collarbone and stunned my whole body for a few seconds. However, before he had time to strike a second time, I moved backwards and out of his reach. I tried to hit him on the side of the head with the canister I had been holding but he moved and the metal object only grazed him. As I retreated, I bumped the plywood shelf, knocking several of the items to the ground and making a racket.

"Stop!" I yelled at the man. But he didn't and grabbed for my neck. Again, I managed to step out of his reach. But before I could get to the gate, he grabbed me from behind. I was almost to the point of passing out when I heard the voice of the woman from the office.

"Mike, let him go!" she hollered.

"I caught him snooping," Mike said, not bothering to loosen his grip on my throat. "Mr. Furman said to . . ."

"It's okay, Mike. I said let him go." After a second or two of pondering the command, the big man loosened his grip around my neck and I could feel the blood gradually returning to my brain.

"I'm sorry, Mr. Norris," the woman from the office said as she hurried across the storage area. "Mike here is responsible for the yard and sometimes he gets a little too excited."

"I noticed," I said, stretching my neck to make sure nothing was broken. "What do you store back here? Gold bullion?"

"No. Just some old parts. We've had a lot of trouble with vandals. Ol' Mike just got a little carried away, that's all. Are you hurt?"

"I'll be okay."

"I'm awfully sorry."

"That's all right," I said, glancing over my shoulder to make sure Mike was a safe distance away from me. The woman walked me to my car. I'm not sure whether she was concerned with my safety or wanted to make sure I left the storage area as quickly as possible. Since I hadn't seen anything that even looked suspicious, I decided to leave before the hired gun with the denim cap had second thoughts.

"Drive carefully back to Jacksonville," she said as I pulled out of the driveway. I think I was more eager to get out of there than she was to see me leave.

As I headed north on Interstate 75, I couldn't help wondering about the incident in the storage area behind Furman's office. Granted, it looked like only a dump area for used parts. But why had that bruiser been so eager to protect a pile of near-worthless junk?

My shoulder still ached where he had slugged me. Just one more reason, I thought, why I should stick to the feature stories and stay away from the investigative stuff. The oldtimers were right. There is no such thing as a seasoned investigative reporter since none of them ever last that long.

9

Eight-thirty, Wednesday morning. One sweet roll and a small glass of orange juice.

The white sandy beach in front of Tony's

hot dog stand was deserted except for the dozen or so seagulls circling the clapboard shack.

Perched precariously on concrete blocks, the "remote restaurant," as he called it, was a primitive affair – a building about twenty-feet square nestled into the sand dunes and a stone's throw from the gently breaking surf. Prices of the various entrees were hand-lettered on the wooden white-washed boards surrounding the formica counter. There was a wooden deck beneath the counter on which were placed about five barstools for the benefit of the customers. And above the opening was a rusted red and blue awning that shook and rattled at the slightest breeze. It was only a half mile south of Hattie's beach house and a great place to stop and catch up on the latest local gossip.

Tony Sinelli purchased the place back in '67 and ran it with the help of his wife and teen-aged daughter. They lived in one of the small houses clustered on the far side of the ocean highway. He was a short pudgy man with tufts of black curly hair surrounding his large protruding ears. In addition to his constant happy demeanor, Tony's subs were considered by locals and visitors alike to be the best south of New Jersey.

The crisp morning air was filled with

the screams of seagulls. About fifty yards offshore, a formation of pelicans flew so close to the water in search of fish, they seemed to almost be admiring their reflections. The warm summer sun grew higher in the sky, burning off the morning dampness. It was the kind of morning for reflecting on one's lifestyle.

"So what's new with you?" Tony asked, taking a sweet roll wrapped in plastic from the microwave oven.

"Same ol' thing," I replied, removing a crumpled dollar bill from my sawed-off blue jeans and sliding it across the counter. "Beach is kind of quiet this morning."

"Yeah. Been this way for the last week or two. Tourists been goin' straight to Disneyworld, I guess. But it'll pick up again soon. Always does."

The sweet roll was warm and tasted good, especially with an orange juice chaser.

If I sound like some kind of health food nut, I don't mean to. While in college, I had my share of beer for breakfast. I can also remember many times when my sole diet for months consisted of hamburgers and Cokes. But after college and intramural sports, the junk food began to catch up and slowly take its toll. About six months after starting with the paper, I felt lousy and decided to take drastic action. I faithfully promised myself to run at least half a mile each day and to cut down on the amount of junk food I eat. In no time, I began feeling better. I love the beach but sitting on the sand and staring out to sea for long periods of time can get a little boring.

"Hey, Tony, any sign of that brunette from Connecticut around here lately? The one with the skimpy white bikini?" Tony shook his head without looking up.

"So what has the big-shot reporter been writing about lately?" he said, waving his trusty spatula in my direction. When I picture Tony, it is always with that spatula in his hand. I doubt if he was capable of talking without it.

"Nothing worth reading," I replied. "Still trying to figure out the Johnson case."

"Oh yeah . . ." he said, a flicker of recognition behind his eyeballs. "I saw in the paper this morning where they found that ol' guy with the fancy ring. You figure he maybe done it?"

"No, but he evidently found the ring. The rest is a mystery."

"Well, I got a theory," Tony continued.

"Save it, Tony," I pleaded. "I've heard it all. And besides, I'd like to forget the whole thing for the moment."

"Suit yourself," he continued, scraping the

141

grease off the grill's black metal surface. "But you remember that murder I solved a couple of months back. You wouldn't believe me that time either, right?"

"At least I'm consistent."

A blue Chevrolet station wagon with New York license plates pulled off the ocean highway and parked on the loose sand. The motor had no sooner been turned off than the mother, father and four children unpacked their beach equipment from the back of the car and headed toward the shore. The father was rather quiet but the mother was arguing with the children in a loud nasal voice coupled with a strong New England accent. My cue to go.

Bathing-suited bodies were beginning to dot the landscape as the barn became visible through the haze. I could make out Hattie's figure walking along the shore in the distance. It was turning into a beautiful day and I was not looking forward to going to work.

"I figured you were probably at Tony's," Hattie said once we were within shouting distance. "You got a phone call from New York about forty-five minutes ago."

"Did they leave a message?"

"Didn't have to. It was that girl you met in Key West. What was her name?"

"Tracy Rogers," I replied, pleased at the

thought she had called. "What did she have to say?"

"Not much. Wanted you to call back. I think she's fishin' for an invite down. She sure didn't waste any time now, did she?" I knew that behind her crusty demeanor, Hattie had taken a liking to the girl from New York.

The phone rang two or three times before the familiar voice on the other end answered.

"Hello, Tracy. What's new in New York?"

"Hi, Brad. I've got some exciting news. At least, it's exciting to me," she replied.

"What's that?"

"One of the syndicates has contracted for me to come down to Jacksonville and work up a feature on your leaping woman story."

"Hey, that's great. When you coming?"

"Tonight. I arrive there at 11.13 P.M. You don't need to meet me, I can take a cab. But I thought you could give me the name of a good hotel down there."

"Nonsense," I replied. "You'll stay with us – we've plenty of room. I'll meet your plane tonight so sit tight in case I'm a little late. I think it's great you got a trip out of this, Tracy, but don't plan on a lot for the moment. The case isn't national news, I'm afraid. At least, not yet."

"Sounds like what you need is a good investigative reporter like me," she said with

143

a giggle. "Now I've got to go and start packing or I'll never make the flight. See you tonight."

"Right," I said, hanging up the receiver. For a few moments, I stared out the sliding glass doors off the kitchen, thinking about Tracy and trying to picture her smile. It had only been a couple of weeks since I had seen her last, although it seemed like months. I wondered if she was genuinely interested in the Johnson case or if it was a scheme to get a free trip to Jacksonville. In any event, I was glad she was coming and looked forward to showing her how romantic a moonlit beach could be.

"Well, she's coming, isn't she?" Hattie said, sounding a bit more like a nagging wife than a landlady. "We've only got the room under the stairs empty and it's full of junk. I'm not giving her my room and you can't expect her to stay in yours!"

"Don't worry, Hattie. She can have my room and I'll sleep on the couch in the living room. We'll get along, no problem. Just wait and see."

"And just how long does she plan to stay with us?"

"She said one of the magazines she writes for assigned her to come down and work up a feature story on the girl that jumped off the

144

bridge. Probably about a week, I guess."

"You guess," Hattie scowled as she walked toward the bathroom. "Crimanelly! I offer to put you up, to keep you from walking the streets and the next thing I know I'm running a motel for transient writers..." Her soliloquy was drowned out by the slamming of the bathroom door upstairs and the running water in the shower.

After fixing a cup of coffee, I again picked up the phone and called homicide.

"Lieutenant Marler's office. May I help you?"

"Yes, is he in?"

"On another line at the moment."

"I'll hold."

"One minute please..."

"This is Marler."

"Hi, Lieutenant. Anything new on the old man yet?"

"Yeah, as a matter of fact, there is. Checking the pawn shops paid off. One of my men found another ring like the one Smith was wearing. The guy said that Smith brought it in about a week ago. Gave him $25 for it."

"Which pawn shop?"

"Aw, hell, I don't remember. Wait a minute, I'll look it up ... here it is. Kessler's Pawn Shop on East 8th Street."

"Thanks," I said, jotting down the address on a notepad. "Anything else?"

"Naw, that's about it."

"Gotten anything back from Lin's office yet?"

"You mean on identifying that ol' guy's clothes and stuff? Not yet. Haven't picked up the final copy of the autopsy yet, either."

"Okay," I said. "Think I'll stop by that pawn shop and snoop around a little on my own. See you this afternoon."

"Yeah, right."

Kessler's Pawn Shop occupied the bottom floor of a two-story building located at the corner of Walnut and East 8th Street. The building was like the once fashionable neighborhood – run down. There were lots of junky items in the front windows: guitars, radios, rifles, space heaters, scissors and knives. A black wire mesh grating covered the windows to keep the local populace from walking away with the merchandise. It did not appear unusual, for all of the businesses in the north end of town had metal bars over the windows and many padlocks on the door. Several even had attack dogs that wandered through the shops at night to discourage prowlers. But to men like Kessler the rising crime rate was not something to become emotional about. It was simply a sign of the

146

times – an indication of things to come – a growing cancer on a wound that had existed for many years.

The front door of the shop tripped a small bell that tinkled, announcing to all that another customer had entered. The windows of the small business were merely a small indication of the interior, for the walls were lined with merchandise reaching all the way to the high ceiling. Used guitars were tied to a metal bar like casings of sausage. And on each side of the narrow shop were glass counters containing hundreds of used items which had probably been brought in many times for a temporary loan.

The store was empty except for a middle-aged black woman who had a young boy by the hand. She appeared to be absently gazing into the glass counters, perhaps looking for a present. The child continued to pivot on the clasped hand, looking about the store and staring with unblinking eyes at my intrusion.

At the rear of the store, a small man was standing behind the counter looking over some sort of inventory sheets. I assumed that he was probably Mr. Kessler, if there was still such a man who owned the business. In square gold wire-framed glasses, he studied the figures on the sheet closely, as if to memorize them. He was only about Hattie's height and appeared to be in his mid-sixties. He wore a shirt with a collar that had never been pressed.

"Good morning," I said.

"Yes, may I help you?" he inquired without looking up from the paper he was studying.

"Brad Norris," I replied. "Wanted to get a little information from you if I could."

"What kind of information were you interested in?" he asked, peering at me over the tops of his spectacles.

"A ring a man brought in about a week ago – gold, with a strange design on the crown."

"Are you with the police department, young man?"

"No, I'm with the morning paper," I replied. "A couple of weeks ago, a Spanish treasure on display at the local art museum was stolen and the police have reason to believe the ring you purchased last week was part of that collection." Marler wouldn't appreciate my putting words in his mouth, but quoting cops sounded a little more formal than a reporter just digging for a good story.

The old man put down his paper and shifted on his stool so that we were facing each other across the scarred glass counter.

"Well, I would like to help you young man, but the police have already been here and they took the ring as evidence. If you want to see it, I'm afraid you'll have to go down to the police station. That's where they have it."

"Thank you," I said, taking the photographs from my coat pocket. "I'll check with them this afternoon. But as long as I'm here, would you mind taking a look at the ring in these photographs and tell me if it's similar to the one you bought from Mr. Smith?"

Kessler held the photographs in his wrinkled hands and pushed his glasses up on the bridge of his nose so he could focus better. After studying the design for a minute or two, he put the pictures on the counter and took off his glasses, rubbing the bridge of his nose with his thumb and index finger.

"Yes, it is similar," he sighed. "You know, it's strange the way he brought it in – the ring, I mean. I think it was on a Wednesday or possibly a Thursday morning. In any event, I remember that it was a rainy, overcast day. Mr. . . . Smith, was it? He had pawned a few items on previous occasions but I didn't remember his name. Anyway, he comes in on this particular morning and he looks in the cases as if he wished to purchase something, you know?"

"Was he by himself?" I asked.

"Oh yes," Kessler replied. "Dressed in this faded old raincoat. Well, he looks around for a while and then I ask if there is anything

149

in particular he is looking for. That's when he approaches me and takes out the ring. However, he doesn't indicate that it might be worth some money but says that it's an heirloom and would I mind holding it for a couple of days."

"Excuse me, sir, but what exactly do you mean that he didn't indicate the value?"

"As I said," Kessler continued, "he told me the ring belonged to his mother and was of nominal value. If the ring is indeed part of the collection that was stolen, then it is made of solid gold and worth many times what I gave him for it. You don't have to be in this business for a lifetime to be able to spot an alcoholic coming down the street. And believe me, Mr. Norris, the people that come in here can squeeze money out of an old Jew like me. I only gave him $25 but he could have easily had a hundred if he wanted it."

"You mean it's as if he didn't want you to know how much the ring was really worth, right?"

"Or didn't know the value himself. He said he only needed the money for a little while and asked that I keep the ring off the main shelf until he could return and purchase it back."

"So he intended to come back," I said, trying to contemplate the man's motives.

"I doubt it," Kessler replied. "Everyone that comes in here only needs the money for a couple of days until their ship comes in. Smith was a deadbeat. I don't think he was any different."

The bell attached to the front door tinkled and a plump woman in her mid forties wearing a print dress and a neckerchief tied around her head stood behind me with a toaster in the crook of her arm. As she argued with Kessler over the relative value of the item, I politely wandered toward a glass case to the side and looked at some chrome pistols with ivory handles he had on display. About three minutes later, the conversation was terminated when the bell of the cash register jingled and Kessler handed the woman three wrinkled dollar bills. She disappeared from the store as quickly as she had come.

"Mr. Kessler, I know that you're busy so I'll be on my way," I said, putting my notepad in my hip pocket. "But you mentioned that Ike Smith had been here before. Can you tell me anything more about him – where he lived or friends he hung around with."

"No, Mr. Norris, I can't. Sure, I'd seen him here and there but where he comes from?" Kessler shook his head. "Who knows where any of these people come from. They don't live, they just exist. Their backgrounds,

151

families, vocations – all behind them. Each day is measured in pints. Nothing else matters – nothing else exists."

"Yes, well thank you for your time," I said, leaving one of my business cards on the counter before turning toward the door. "I would appreciate it if you would call me at the paper if you can think of anything else."

"One place you might try is down at the docks," Kessler said behind me. "Seems to me that Smith had an in with one of the men down there and got jobs sweeping out the warehouses from time to time. You know, make enough to tide him over when the going got tough."

"Okay. Happen to know the contact?"

"No, but the crew that hangs around down there is usually the same. They can tell you."

The twelve o'clock whistle was blowing for lunch when I pulled the Mustang off the dusty industrial highway that ran parallel to the river and into the parking lot of the Port Authority docks.

Built in the early 19th century and originally known as "Cowford," the city of Jacksonville owes its rapid growth to shipping. Until railroads and eventually airplanes connected remote portions of Florida and Georgia with the industrialized

152

North, Jacksonville was the commercial hub through which all supplies moved. It was also the means by which tourists came to Florida from the northern states in order to sit out the winter months. Jacksonville still receives annual revenues in the millions of dollars from the vast number of ships that moor up to her many docks each day.

There are several oil refineries and industries that own riverfront land and maintain their own docking facilities. However, the largest stevedore operation through which most goods entering and leaving Jacksonville pass is owned and operated by the city in cooperation with local steamship companies. Each company maintains its own warehouses but the overall operation is administered by the Jacksonville Port Authority and city employees.

I doubted if any of the executives would know anything about Ike Smith so I decided instead to pay a visit to Mike Webb, head of the local mariner's union. His office was located on the first floor of the administration building inside the front gate.

"Hello, Mike. How are you?"

"Fine, Brad," he said, shaking my hand vigorously. "Where you been? Hiding? How come you don't visit us more often?"

"Who are you kidding? You know damn

153

good and well the only time you want me around is when you're ready to make a press release at negotiation time and not until. Glad to see you're still pumping out the same ol' bull, though," I joked.

I got to know Mike fairly well when the dockworkers went on strike a year and a half ago. He is definitely a graduate of the old school, worked his way up from the wharf the hard way. But he's a fair man and looks out for the welfare of the men he represents.

Leaning back in his padded swivel chair, Mike put a Viceroy in the plastic cigarette holder he always used to cut down on the amount of tar. His deep gravelly voice added to the overall tough image he liked to portray. But away from the bargaining table, he was a pretty sensitive guy.

"So what brings you snooping around the docks this time?" Mike said, blowing smoke in my direction.

"Trying to run down this fellow named Ike Smith who was killed in the hotel fire yesterday. Did you ever hear of him?"

"Smith," he mumbled, letting the name sink into his memory. "No, I can't say that I do. Why do you want to know?"

"He might be tied into this story I'm working on. This is a picture of the guy that one of our photographers took at the fire," I said, removing the black and white pictures from my pocket. "How about looking at them and see if you recognize him?"

"Sure," he said, taking the pictures from my hand. "Man, he was burned pretty bad, wasn't he? I doubt even his mother would recognize him." Mike studied the pictures for a moment and then handed them back. "Sorry, Brad, but I can't say as I've ever laid eyes on 'em. I know he isn't a member of the union but if you like, I'll check the register just to make sure," he said, taking the booklet from the bottom right hand drawer of his battered wooden desk. "Nope. No Ike Smith listed here."

"Well, it was worth a try. I was just over at a pawn shop on 8th Street and the guy said he understood that Smith would sweep out one of the warehouses when he needed money."

"That's still possible," Mike continued. "Although the docks are union, the contract does allow each shipping company to hire spot labor for grunt jobs like sweeping the floor and stuff like that. You'd have to go to each warehouse and ask around, though. I can't help you there."

"Okay, but I'd appreciate it if you'd keep your ears open."

"Will do. What story is this anyway?"

"Smith was wearing a ring that may have been one of the items taken during the robbery of the museum not long ago," I replied.

"Hey, isn't that the one where that woman was killed jumping off the bridge?"

"Yep, that's the one."

"I heard the guys talking about that on the wharf. Rumor has it she didn't jump."

"Thought of that myself, Mike. Except a cop watched her go over the side and there was no other way off the bridge other than down."

"Maybe so. But all I know is what I hear," Mike said knocking the remains of his cigarette into the ashtray.

"You know, the woman worked for the Mediterranean Maritime Company. Got anything on them?"

Mike reamed out the plastic holder with a bent up old pipe cleaner he took from his desk.

"Same as all the rest, I guess. A guy named Hall runs the local office. Ran a branch in Europe before he came here. They handle a lot of companies in the Med – Italy, Greece, the like. Employ about thirty or forty people here. That's about all I know."

"Something tells me that's where Ike

Smith's name will pop up. At least I hope so."

Mike got up from behind his desk to see me to the door. "If you don't have any luck there, you might ask around at that old bar across the street, the Sailor's Delight. If this Smith worked on the docks, then he probably spent most of his paycheck in that place. Most of 'em do."

"Thanks," I said. "I'll keep in touch."

Checking around the wharf didn't provide a lot in the way of information. A few of the people I talked to recognized the face and said they had seen Smith around the wharf but weren't quite sure whom he worked for. One of the foremen at the Mediterranean Maritime Company said Smith had cleaned up their warehouse on occasion but hadn't been around in about two months. I tried to question him further but he said I would have to get any further information from Mr. Hall.

Leaving the docks about 3 P.M., I stopped at the bar across the street. It was a small rundown building covered with weathered brown shingles and a small addition for the toilet added on behind. The front porch sagged from the years of wear and Christmas tree lights were strung from beneath the eaves although it was the middle of summer. The cramped atmosphere of the place was muggy and smelled of stale beer. A bar ran the length of the wall closest to the door and was lined with about ten vinyl bar stools. About four wooden tables filled the rest of the room with the wooden chairs tilted against the sides of the tables.

Behind the bar was a large mirror with bottles of rum, whiskey and vodka lined up on the three shelves. A big gold-leafed cash register was on the middle of the top shelf with several snapshots of children and a woman in a bikini taped around it. The room was empty except for a heavy set woman tending bar and two men in oily workclothes sipping beers on bar stools at the corner of the bar.

After ordering a bottle of beer, I sat on a stool nearest the door and attempted to engage the woman in a conversation. She was pleasant enough but didn't appear too interested in making friendships. In the interest of saving time, I took the photograph of Smith from my pocket and asked her if she had ever seen the old man around.

"Not in a long while," she said, looking at the photo I still held in my hand. "Yeah, he used to come in with the rest of them on payday. But I don't remember anything unusual about him, if that's what you mean. He never tore the place up or took off without paying. He'd just come in when he had some money and drink it up."

"Did he ever come in with anybody in particular?" I asked.

"Naw, just the usual crowd. At least if he did, I don't remember. Sorry," she said as she resumed wiping down the mahogany bar with a damp rag. "You might ask the guys at the bar there. Maybe they seen him."

One of the men was tall and thin and wore a long billed work cap which was covered with layers of grease. The second wore bib overalls dirtier than the first man's hat, if that was possible.

"Sure, I knows him," said the man with the hat. "That there's ol' Ike Smith. He was killed yesterday, you know."

"Yes, I know," I replied. "Where did you know him from? Did you work with him?"

"Oh yeah," the man replied. "Whenever ol' Ike was short on money, the man would hire him to sweep out the place. But he hadn't come around in a while. He was staying at the Ashton, so I guess he was doing all right for hisself."

"You say he was hired to clean the place. What place was that?" I asked.

"The Med warehouse," the man replied. "When he got desperate, he'd come around all right and the man, he'd let Ike sweep up and clean out the toilets. Ike do real good, too. Good worker when he have a mind to."

"What man is that?"

"The foreman. One time Ike told me he had a daughter who knew the foreman and put in a good word for him. Must be true 'cause the place get a little messy and the man not have us clean it waiting for ol' Ike to come around. Yes sir, he was a damn good worker when he have a mind to."

"The daughter. You wouldn't happen to know the name of his daughter, would you?"

"Nope. He never talked about her," replied the man with the hat. " 'Ceptin' for the time he mentioned she knows the man. But he did say she done all right for herself. Had a high school degree and everything!"

"Does she live in Jacksonville?"

"As far as I knows, she does."

"Tell me, when was the last time you saw Ike?"

"Oh, it got to be at least a month. Ran into him downtown and we drank a few together. But I ain't seen him since. I was real sorry to see where he died and all. He was okay, you know?"

"Right," I replied, taking a business card from my shirt pocket. "If you hear anything, give me a call, will you? There's a six pack in it for you if you turn up anything worth while."

"You got it," the laborer said with a wide grin. "The minute's I run across somethin', you'll be the first to hear it."

It was approaching dinner time as I stepped into the muddy parking lot of the waterfront bar. The thought of Tracy flying into town flashed through my mind. I was looking forward to her company. But her arrival was seven hours away and there were things to do.

The police parking lot was nearly empty as I drove the Mustang up to the building and parked next to an orange and yellow pickup truck with the words STATE DIVISION OF BRIDGES AND HIGHWAYS painted on the door.

Most of the detectives were gone from homicide and the door to Marler's office was closed, indicating that he had someone in there. Settling behind the secretary's desk, I dialed the phone number of the medical examiner's office.

"Hello, Dr. Lin?"

"Yes."

"Brad Norris here. Have you completed the autopsy on Smith?"

"Oh yes. One of Lt. Marler's men picked

it up about an hour ago. You might check with . . ."

"I'm in his office now," I replied. "Were there any surprising results?"

"No, I wouldn't say so. Judging from the poor state of his liver and other vital signs, we concluded that Mr. Smith was a very heavy drinker and was suffering from a tumor of the prostate. However, it was in the formative stages, so I doubt if it caused any pain."

"Has anyone inquired about the body yet?" I asked.

"Well, er . . . ah, no. Should there be? I didn't think he had any relatives," Lin asked over the phone.

"Neither did I until about an hour ago. One of his drinking buddies down at the wharf said he had a daughter who lived nearby. However, he didn't know her name or anything else about her. So I was kind of hoping maybe she had read about his death in the paper and had come to collect his body."

"No, there haven't been any inquiries that I know about. But thanks for letting me know. I'm planning on leaving soon but I'll brief my assistant to be on the look out tonight."

As I started to dial the number of the city desk, the door to Marler's office opened and Stuart Eisenberg appeared, smoking his

Algerian Briar pipe and leaving a trail of smoke behind him.

"Hello, Mr. Eisenberg. I thought that truck in the parking lot rang a bell," I said, looking up from the desk. "I noticed the special configuration on the back. Tell me, do you use special equipment when you inspect those bridges?"

"I don't know whether you'd call it special or not. But yes, there are various types of equipment we use on occasion," he answered, sucking on the plastic stem he gripped between his teeth.

"Equipment to go over the side of a bridge?"

"Yes, there's a seat known as a bosun's chair which can be used. But it's nothing more than a small leather seat which is lowered by means of ropes and pulleys. And we very rarely use it. Why do you ask?"

"Oh, nothing really. Just a thought."

"Well, if you don't mind, he didn't come up here to talk with you," Marler said from the doorway of his office. Eisenberg continued to stare at me for a moment as if to ask a question but then took advantage of Marler's cue and continued out the door and into the hallway.

"Where do you think he fits it, Lieutenant?"

"Aw, he ain't involved," Marler said, shrugging his shoulders and turning to walk back into his office. "Just wanted to go over a few things with him, that's all. And why all the questions about the equipment he uses?"

"Well, I thought that maybe the girl lowered herself to the water's edge using something like that."

"Oh hell, we thought of that two weeks ago. Two problems though. First, they don't make anything that can lower a person one hundred fifty feet in fifteen seconds. And furthermore, who untied the rope on the railing when she got to the bottom?"

"Can't blame me for asking. By the way, those rags you found under the bridge. Did you tie them to Smith?"

"Yep, I guess you could say so. There were some hairs that matched his. And an empty can of Sterno had his prints all over it. But all it does is tie him to the area. We still don't know how he came across the bag or what he did with the rest of the jewels."

"And you were hoping maybe Eisenberg remembered something that might help, huh?"

"Unless you got some better ideas," he said, taking a cigarette from the pack on his desk and lighting one up.

"I'm afraid I don't, Lieutenant. But I did

164

run across some information this afternoon I think you might be interested in."

"What kind of information?"

"Well, for starters, Ike Smith used to make some occasional money sweeping up the Mediterranean Maritime Company warehouse over at the main docks. Seemed he had a working relationship with one of the foremen over there."

"Vicki Johnson's old employer, right?"

"And the same place that money bag came from, don't forget."

"Hmm. Interesting but doesn't tell us a lot. That it?"

"Nope. One of the longshoremen that knew Ike said he once told this guy he had a daughter who set him up with the foreman."

"Got a name?"

"No name. He didn't seem to know anything else about her either except that she lived in Jacksonville, or so he thought."

"I better notify Lin in case she tries to claim the body," Marler said.

"Save your breath, Lieutenant. I already did. But you might run a federal check on Smith in Washington and see if they can turn up anything. Seems like that shipping company has popped up too many times to be coincidental, don't you think?"

"Perhaps," Marler said, "but not necessarily. You can print whatever you like but I'm not jumping to any conclusions. Not yet, anyways."

"Yeah, well, if you're tired of looking at my face, wait until tomorrow. A friend of mine is flying in from New York to do a feature on this story. How about that? You'll be a national celebrity before you know it."

"Great, just what I need! Another one of you following me around with your little notepads," he said, stamping out the butt of his cigarette in the little ceramic ashtray on the corner of his desk. "You know, my wife is right. I should go for early retirement and buy that trailer camp down in Ft. Lauderdale."

"What, and give all this up? You'd be back in a month, Lieutenant."

"Don't bank on it, Norris. Nothing could be prettier than looking at Jacksonville in the rear view mirror of my car!"

Tracy's flight was only twenty-five minutes late – just enough time for a couple of rounds in the airport lounge.

"Welcome to Florida again," I said, providing her with a kiss on the cheek and reaching out to take the flight bag she carried in one hand.

166

"Thanks. It's nice to be back – and so soon!"

"Have a good flight?"

"The usual," she replied as we made our way downstairs to the baggage pickup area. "So what's new since I last saw you?"

"Not much, I'm afraid. What you've heard about the South is true, you know. Same thing that happens in the North only slower."

"Very funny," she smiled, "but I'm not buying that old 'Uncle Remus' routine. Fill me in on the Johnson case, will you?"

"With you looking as good as you do? Not a chance. I've heard enough of that case to last me a while. And besides, there's plenty of time to bring you up to date later. Let's pick up your bags and we'll go have a drink and talk over new times, what say?"

Following the forty-five minute drive to the beach from the airport and a drink or two on the way, I took Tracy for a walk on the moonlit beach and attempted to show her how hospitable Floridians can be.

"Brad, it's even prettier than Key West," she said as we walked barefoot in the wet sand. Her hand felt warm and comfortable in mine as we passed Tony's stand which was closed.

"I don't think I could ever leave Florida, Tracy. You get so addicted to this weather. I don't know how people can come down here for a week or two in the middle of winter and then go home facing all that snow and cold. I don't make as much money as I probably could further north. But I feel living here is a pretty good tradeoff."

After reaching a deserted portion of the beach, Tracy and I sat down near a sand dune and watched the moonlight as it reflected off the crashing waves.

"I missed you, Brad."

"The thought of you crossed my mind more than once, Tracy." Without another word, she leaned over and kissed me passionately on the lips. The memory of our lovemaking in Key West suddenly rushed to my senses. I enjoyed her more than anyone I had ever known and I wondered if she felt the same about me.

A gentle wind blew in off the Atlantic and rustled a clump of seaoats growing behind where we were sitting. About fifty yards to the south, I could make out the figures of several dozen seagulls nesting on the beach. It was a tranquil scene. And having Tracy there in my arms made it all complete.

As we rolled around in the privacy of the darkness, all worldly thoughts were pushed from our minds. It was a very special moment for both of us and we tried to make it last as long as we could.

10

"Max, this is Tracy Rogers, a friend of mine from New York. She'll be here for about a week working up a feature on the Johnson case."

Schuman nodded his balding head in Tracy's direction but didn't extend his hand. His gaze quickly turned toward me and the look in his eyes was far from pleasant. "I'm sure she'll be able to put together a better story than you have without much effort. Every other news agency in town has."

"Cheap shot," I said, knowing full well what he was talking about. "Nobody else in town has beat us on the story."

"No argument there," Max continued. "But I put Hastings on regular police beat two weeks ago so you could work this case full time. I was hoping for some more dramatic stuff than the pap you've been dragging in here. At least a couple of blazing headlines once in a while would be nice," he said,

169

waving his arms as he did whenever he got excited. "You know, something like 'Leaping Bandit Still in Hiding?' Something with a little pizzazz that might help us sell a few papers would be a welcome change."

"Aw, come on Max. You can only run speculation without a body for so long," I replied, raising my voice a little in hopes of possibly intimidating him a bit. Tracy had backed away a few paces and pretended to be memorizing the bulletin board. "They just haven't come up with anything good enough to print yet. The only thread so far is this Ike Smith character."

"Fine. We'll just run an ad telling folks to hold out for the book!"

"Cute. Real cute," I said. "Just sit tight for another couple of days and they're bound to turn up her body. Then you'll have your A-1 story, promise."

"Norris, I've given you all the time and money you need on this story. You get scooped on this one and you'll be doing obits the rest of your life, you got that?"

"Yeah, I got it." Nothing like a good healthy butt chewing to get the juices flowing. While Max took the opportunity to catch his breath, I grabbed Tracy by the arm and headed for the employee cafeteria downstairs. Suddenly, a tall glass of Maalox with an orange juice chaser sounded awfully good.

"Is he always that pleasant?" Tracy asked, taking a seat near the window overlooking the courtyard.

"Only when he's in a good mood," I replied.

"Aren't you a little worried – about getting scooped, I mean?"

"No, not really. He just worries a lot. Everybody else in town has been taking their stuff right out of my columns. Nobody's going to scoop me unless by luck."

"So allow me to ask the $64,000 question. How come they haven't run across the body yet?"

"Your guess is as good as mine. One man I talked to said he thought the body might have snagged on some underwater debris. Probably fish food by now."

"Clothes too?" Tracy asked.

"Except for that strip of cloth on the riverbank that supposedly matched her outfit. But how it got there or what happened to the rest is anybody's guess."

"I think the mystery actually makes for a better story, don't you?"

"Maybe for your magazine, love. But newspapers don't deal in those kind of headlines," I added. "The guy reading the morning paper over breakfast isn't interested in hypothetical situations – he just wants the facts. If he wants plots, he can go for Sherlock Holmes. The average reader would just as soon you leave the question marks out."

"Sounds like a lot of boring writing to me."

"Formula writing, that's for sure. Boring? I guess the really exciting stories only come along about ten percent of the time. But there are worse averages in life, I guess."

I saw Wink McCormick walk through the food line with a sandwich and Coke and waved for him to come and join us.

"This is Tracy Rogers, Wink," I said as he sat down at our table. "Flew down from New York to cover the Johnson story for one of her magazines."

"Howdy," Wink said, flashing a wide smile and sticking out his large black hand. "Hope your trip wasn't wasted."

"Thanks," Tracy said. "I'm sure it won't be. Based on what Brad has told me, it sounds like an interesting enough tale."

"Maybe for her magazine," I continued, directing my conversation toward Wink, "but Max just gave me the word. Either I stop putting the city desk to sleep with my coverage or I get to fly home with Tracy here on a permanent basis!"

"You'll get no arguments from me," Tracy followed with a smile.

"Speaking of missing bodies, I was developing some film in the darkroom just now and heard a twenty-six on the scanner," Wink said between bites of his sandwich.

"What's a twenty-six?" Tracy asked.

"That's a drowning," I replied, still looking at Wink. "Remember the location?"

"Yeah. Robinson Lake. Body was found floating near the bank about a half hour ago. I was on the westside shooting some pictures for advertising and had just come back. When I heard the call, I was going to drive out and burn a roll but Jacobs called in on the car radio and said he would stop on the way in. He should probably have some good shots if you can work some decent cutlines out of it."

"Me," I stammered. "What about Hastings? He's supposed to be covering police while I'm working this other thing. Why don't they send him out?"

"Man, you become a real prima donna lately, ain't you?" Wink said with a needling grin. "I don't care if nobody goes out. Just thought you might like to know. I believe Hastings is at the beach working up a story on the union negotiations. I didn't realize your schedule was so booked up."

"Okay," I said. "Point made. I'll drive out and have a look. You want to come along or stay here, Tracy?"

173

"Count me in," she replied, pulling the strap of her large leather purse over her shoulder.

Traffic was light as we pulled out of the employee parking lot.

"Where is this Robinson Lake anyway?"

"An old landfill site west of town," I answered, pushing down the accelerator of the Chevrolet assigned to the police reporter. "Past the military base, it's about a twenty minute drive."

"I take it you know the area fairly well."

"I've been there once or twice. It's a good fishing spot. People out that way like to fish there on the weekend and drink a little beer. And from time to time, a body turns up. Sometimes they get a little too drunk and fall in the water. And sometimes it involves a little foul play."

The concrete and stucco houses that lined the expressway were a blur as we passed them on our way to the Westside lake.

"Doesn't sound like Jacksonville is a very safe place to live," Tracy said.

"I don't know about that. I'd say it is probably as safe as any other medium-sized city. What are the figures? About eighty percent of all people murdered are crimes of passion. You're safe as long as you travel in the right crowd."

174

"You know, I've never been in Jacksonville before."

"Really? It's not a bad place to live," I continued. "The only place in Florida where you can still get a change of seasons. Has the best of both worlds too, I guess. The population is about three quarters of a million but it's still pretty much a small town atmosphere. Lots of streets but they still roll 'em up at night."

"After living in New York, that can be a real blessing."

About five miles past the military base, we came to the dirt road that led to Robinson Lake. Surrounded by trees, the lake is set back fifty yards from the four-lane highway and is well-concealed. A visitor would miss the turn unless they knew where to look.

Several police and rescue vehicles were parked among the trees and along the grassy banks of the lake. People in various uniforms were grouped at one corner of the five-acre lake. Since it was a Thursday, few fishermen were in the area. I checked my watch as we got out of the car and walked toward the men. It was almost 2 P.M. A warm and gentle breeze rustled through the tops of the pine trees and over the dark brown surface of the water.

Two attendants from the medical
175

examiner's office were putting the badly decomposed body of a young woman into a thick canvas body bag as we joined the group. I could tell it was a woman by the long hair which hung toward the ground and was matted from the dried algae. Tracy preferred to stay several yards away while I elbowed my way up to Marler who was observing the whole thing from a spot near the rear of the medical examiner's station wagon.

"Identified her yet?"

"Are you kidding? Did you see her face? We had a hard enough time determining whether it was even human," he said.

"Any sign of foul play?"

"I didn't see any," Marler continued. "No bullet holes that we could find. But we'll have to wait and see what Lin says to be sure."

"How about witnesses?" I asked.

"The guy over there in the blue plaid shirt and jeans discovered the body this morning."

"How long you figure she's been in there?"

"Hard to say. Maybe as long as a month. We're hoping Lin can tell us a little more."

"Month, huh? How could she be in a lake this small without somebody spotting the body, you reckon?"

Marler shrugged his shoulders but did not answer. With the body in the bag and strapped into place, the attendants put the metal stretcher into the back of the station wagon. Several of the police and firemen who answered the call were breaking into smaller groups and beginning to drift away. I caught out of the corner of my eye a couple of younger cops who had spotted Tracy and were in the process of trying to give her exclusive interviews.

"About how old, Lieutenant?" I said, notepad in hand.

"I dunno. Early twenties maybe. About five feet six, average weight. That's about all we know right now."

"Okay, I'll check with Lin a little later," I replied, making my way toward the cowboy who had first stumbled across the body. He had been staring at his shiny leather boots for the last couple of minutes, but had finally realized he was no longer needed for questioning and started walking toward his yellow pickup truck parked beneath a clump of pine trees.

"Excuse me but could I talk with you for a second?" He didn't bother to answer but froze in his tracks. "I understand you're the one that found the body this morning. Could you tell me a little about it?"

"Ain't much to tell, really," he said with a distinct southern accent and a wad of chewing tobacco concealed in his cheek. "I come here a' fishin' every now and then. Well sir, bout noon when I parked my truck right thar 'neath them trees and walked to that there spot on the bank. That's when I first seen her." He pointed with a bony index finger to the area where the bank was still wet.

"I see. And where was the body when you first spotted it?" I asked, making a few notations on my pad.

"Right thar. It had just washed up in the shallow part and was just a'layin thar face down. I didn't touch it, no sir! Just turned around and gets the hell out of here. Called the po-lice straight away. Don't wants nothing to do with this mess, understand?"

"Anybody else around at the time?"

"W'all, thar was a negra couple on the far bank a fishin," he continued. "But I reckon that was it. I shore didn't waste no time gettin outta here once I saw that the woman a floatin in the water weren't no swimmer, no sir."

After taking the man's name and address, I made my way over to Marler who was jotting a few notes of his own and talking to one of his detectives. Tracy had already introduced herself and was listening to the conversation as I joined them.

"How do we stand on the Johnson case today? Anything new?" I asked.

"Nothing," Marler replied.

"You know, my editor is riding me pretty heavy, Lieutenant. If I'm going to keep my job, we're going to have to start turning over a lot more rocks."

"We? Since when do I work for you?"

"Aw, you know what I mean," I replied, obviously not my day for striking up conversations. "It would sure help if you'd fill me in on what you have."

"Hell, Norris, you know more than half my men. But don't worry. Unofficially, you get first shot at what we got when we get it. So far, we got nothing so just relax and sit quiet for a while."

"Sit on Max? You don't know what you're asking. Any word from Washington yet on Ike Smith's background?"

"None yet. Maybe something this afternoon." With that, Marler stuffed his notebook into the pocket of his coat and walked toward his green Dodge nearby. The other detectives followed suit and started to clean up the area. I walked to the edge of the water and Tracy followed, clutching her spiral notepad as if for security. The water was dark and the bottom was invisible two feet from shore. The wind caused tiny ripples of water to lap against the muddy bank where the woman's body had been discovered.

"How deep is this lake, anyway?"

179

"I don't know," I replied. "Forty, maybe fifty feet. Deep enough to drown in."

"Poor girl," Tracy said with a sigh.

"Yeah, tough. That's the way it happens sometimes." I squatted by the edge of the water in hopes of discovering something the police might have missed. "We know that she was a white woman and young. And judging from the style of clothing she was wearing, she wasn't from this neighborhood and probably not the type to come here often."

"What's that?"

"Clothes were too nice. No designer fashions, mind you. But still a cut above what the average fisherman would wear out here. We'll have to wait and see what Doc Lin has to say. If there's foul play involved, I'll bet she was out here parked with a boyfriend, they got into an argument and he did her in."

"Got it all figured out, don't you?"

"Wait and see. I've been on this beat long enough not to need a crystal ball. They all happen the same – just different faces, that's all."

"You're on. Now, if you've gotten all you need, what do you say we split," Tracy said. "This place gives me the creeps."

Upon returning to the newsroom, I gave Tracy a list of phone numbers to call while

I paid another visit to the office of the Mediterranean Maritime Company.

Vicki Johnson's desk had been completely cleared since my last visit. The same middle-aged secretary was still at her desk, typing invoices and occasionally answering the phone. The other woman who worked there was absent and her desk was neatly arranged as if to indicate she hadn't been in that day. Mr. Hall was studying some reports spread across his mahogany desk and didn't notice me standing in the doorway until I cleared my throat.

"Hello Mr. Hall. Brad Norris of the *Chronicle*," I said, barging into the small office and not bothering to wait for an invite. His eyes mirrored his disgust at my presence but he only stared as I slipped into the small padded chair facing him from across the desk.

"Mr. Norris, I'm afraid . . ."

"I know you're busy, sir," I continued, "but there are just a few questions I'd like to ask first. Have you ever heard of a man named Ike Smith?"

"I don't believe so. Should I?"

"I understand he has worked in your waterfront warehouse on several occasions. Would you have any record of him in your personnel files?"

"Yes, we should have. Is he working there now?"

"No, I'm afraid he's dead. But I don't believe he ever worked there full time, anyway – just a day or two at a time."

"Well, he should still be listed in our tax records if he worked during this past year." Mr. Hall turned and in a loud voice, asked the secretary sitting outside the open doorway to bring the folder containing the employee W-2 forms. After staring at the records through a pair of bifocals for several minutes, he looked up and shook his head.

"There's a Willie Smith, Randall Smith – several Smiths, in fact. But no Ike Smith, I'm afraid. Here, you can see for yourself," he said, turning the folder around and pushing it across the desktop. "Perhaps he went by another name? A lot of them do that to cheat on income tax. Do you have another name?"

"No. Ike Smith is about all we have to go on for the time being."

"Have you talked with our foreman in the warehouse?"

"Not yet," I replied. "I was down there yesterday but he was out at the time. That's my next stop, though. By the way, I see you have cleaned away Miss Johnson's things. Has anyone stopped by to pick them up?"

"We turned everything over to the police,"

Hall said, standing up and hoping I would follow suit. "I don't believe she had any family, Mr. Norris. None that I'm aware of anyway."

"How about benefits? Did she have any pay coming?"

"That's company business, Mr. Norris. However, I will tell you Miss Johnson was paid in full at the time of her death. She received a pay check the last day before going on vacation."

"Vacation? What vacation? I didn't know she was on vacation," I babbled, suddenly feeling nauseated – a feeling I get whenever I trip over something and wonder how many countless millions of other slobs are already aware of the same secret.

"Miss Johnson went on vacation the week before she disappeared," he continued, a little perturbed with the new line of questioning. "She was due back to work the Monday following the incident."

"Did she say where she was going?"

"South Florida I believe. But nothing specific. The last time any of us saw her was the Friday before. We all wished her a nice time and looked forward to seeing her in a week. I certainly got the impression she was coming back. But then one never knows."

"Mr. Hall, a bridge inspector discovered

183

the bank deposit bag yesterday with your company's emblem on it and a coin from the stolen collection inside. Any idea where it came from?"

Hall led me out of his office and to a desk near the front door. Opening one of the desk drawers, he took out four or five bags that were identical to the bag discovered by Eisenberg the day before. "The banks provide these for their best customers, Mr. Norris. If Miss Johnson was involved in this thing, it would have been very easy to use one of these. Or someone just as easily could have walked through that door and helped themselves to one of these while the secretaries were away from their desks."

"Possible, but a little too coincidental, don't you think? Did she mention any friends?"

"I believe you asked me that question before," Hall said as he closed the desk drawer and inched me toward the front of the office. "As I told you then, her personal life was kept private and we didn't violate it here. I believe she was dating an older man but I don't know his name or anything about him. I have no idea what he looks like or even where you might look."

"Yes, well, thanks for your time. What was the name of the foreman, again?"

"Callahan. Patrick Callahan," he said,

closing the front door with the white venetian blinds behind me. The waterfront warehouse was about 10 blocks north on Meyer Street and only a few minutes drive. This time, one of the workers pointed to the foreman standing near the shipping desk.

Callahan stood about five feet eight inches tall and was stocky. He was wearing a plaid shirt and green workpants which covered the tops of his heavy boots. His long wavy hair was almost the color of strawberries and the sensitive white skin was also evident, despite his masculine features. I walked up behind him and waited until he was through with what he was doing before interrupting.

"Mr. Callahan, I wonder if I might talk with you a moment?"

"What d'ya want to talk about?" he said, putting a clipboard under his arm and a chewed-up pencil behind his ear.

"Ike Smith. I understand he used to work down here from time to time." As I talked, a convoy of tow motors whizzed by with loads of goods being unloaded off a ship and stored inside the warehouse. The foreman began walking toward a door which opened onto the loading wharf and I continued alongside, talking as we went.

"Yeah, he worked around here from time to time. So what else you need to know?"

185

"It looks like he's tied up in this robbery and suicide thing. He was wearing a stolen ring when they found his body the other day."

"Naw, can't be," Callahan continued. "Not Ike. That ol' man was so slow he could hardly push a broom. How they figure he could have knocked off that place?"

"I don't think they believe he was involved in the actual robbery. But he might have found the bag on the riverbank. We've tied him to the area."

"So what's that got to do with us?"

"I talked to a longshoreman yesterday who told me Ike got work down here because his daughter knew the foreman. Then I went to Hall's office just a few minutes ago and checked the records but found no Ike Smith listed."

"If I talk t'ya, you gonna keep your mouth shut?"

"I promise to leave your name out of it," I replied. Callahan continued to walk along the edge of the dock for a couple of minutes. He didn't say anything but just stared out over the river.

"Ike's daughter was Vicki Johnson," he said, his hands tucked into the back pockets of his pants. He did not look at me but continued to study the ripples on the water's

186

surface. "You won't find his name on the company records cause it's against policy for more'n one member of a family to work for Maritime. Paid 'em out of my pocket, or rather hers. But ol' Ike never knew. The other men there, they knew the score and went along with it."

"How well did you know Vicki Johnson?"

"I didn't know her very well. She used to bring paperwork down here and a couple of times a week I'd stop by the office with waybills. Her ol' man was a good sport – he loved his rum all right. But he was a likable sort. Had a little pension he lived on but about every other month he'd drink that up and need a few extra dollars to tide him over. So she'd call me and tell me he was comin' and I'd let him push a broom around for a couple of hours. Now you print that and ol' man Hall will fire me as sure as I'm standing here."

"Was his real name Johnson?"

"No, but it wasn't Smith either. He just used that to beat the taxes. I don't remember his real name. Most of us just knew him as Ike."

"When was the last time you saw him?" I asked.

"Been at least a month or two," he said, looking me over out of the corner of his eye.

"Sometimes, I understand, he'd drift down to Miami or over toward Tampa when the mood hit'm. I just figured he'd gone on one of his traveling trips."

"How about the girl? Why do you think she did it? Hard up for money, maybe?"

"Can't answer that one. She seemed like a pretty nice person to me. But then who really knows what's inside another person's heart?" Callahan took his hands out of his back pockets and crossed his arms over his broad chest.

"Friends. Did she ever talk about friends?"

"Like I told you, I didn't know her that well. Drove her home once when her car was being fixed and met a girlfriend of hers. But I don't remember her name so I guess that doesn't help you much."

"Did she live in the same apartment as Vicki?"

"Don't think she ever said. She was pretty, though. I remember that. Had blonde hair and big blue eyes – real pretty girl, all right." Callahan turned away from the water and began walking back toward the warehouse. "Listen, it's been real nice talking with you but I gotta get back to work. You just make sure you keep what I told you quiet, hear?"

"Okay, but it doesn't fit," I said, trying to pursue the questioning. "The girl turns

188

up missing, then Ike apparently stumbles across the treasure and then he turns up dead. Somehow he must have discovered that treasure after she jumped. Which means she may still be alive."

"Your guess is as good as mine," Callahan said. "He didn't have a place really – slept wherever he got the urge. I know that Vicki Johnson wasn't too crazy about his drinking and wouldn't put up with his shenanigans. He was a proud ol' fool though – wouldn't take charity. She had to set up the work scheme in order to keep his belly full of something besides wine."

"He must have been in this thing with her. Otherwise, he wouldn't have known where to look. Unless, of course, Vicki is still alive – which is starting to look more and more possible."

"If that's what you think. Like I said, the Vicki Johnson I knew wasn't into that sort of thing. She was too nice a person for anything like stealing. I can't imagine her stealing anything, let alone jumping off a bridge like that. Nope, what happened is beyond me – none of it makes any sense."

My next stop after leaving the warehouse was the Sand Flea Apartments on Post Street – the complex where Vicki Johnson and Gail Tomlinson lived. The elderly gray-haired

189

woman who managed the apartment house said the police had sealed off the missing girl's apartment following her disappearance and left strict orders that no one be allowed to enter without permission. I decided pursuing it wasn't worth the hassle.

Before leaving the Sand Flea, however, I went to Gail Tomlinson's apartment to leave a note telling her I wouldn't be able to keep our date Friday night. Figuring she would be at work, I rang the bell twice as I scribbled a message on my notepad just in case I might be wrong and she was home. I was wrong. After a minute, the front door opened a crack to reveal her familiar face. Her streaked blonde hair was rather disheveled and she was dressed in faded blue jeans and a loose white blouse. It was rather obvious that she hadn't been to work that day.

"Hello, Gail," I said. "Hope I didn't catch you sleeping?"

"Er ... uh, hello," she stammered. Whatever she was up to, I had definitely caught her off guard. "Uh yes, as a matter of fact, I was resting ... think I've picked up a cold or something."

"Sorry to hear it," I replied. "I just wanted to tell you that I wouldn't be able to keep our date Friday night. A friend flew in from out of town unexpectedly. Maybe another time?"

"Yes, another time would be nice," she said, not bothering to open the door any wider than she already had.

"Gail, I don't mean to intrude but could I use your phone for just a moment?" I could tell by her expression that she would have liked to have refused my request but couldn't without raising suspicions. She opened the door far enough to allow me to slip inside and then closed it quickly behind me.

"You'll find it over there on the wall," she added, pointing in the direction of the kitchen.

"Thanks," I replied. "You know you may have that A-strain that's been going around. Understand it lasts for a couple of days before the fever breaks." Gail had already slipped onto the living room couch while I called the office and checked in with Max. She was holding her head in one hand when I came out. Even without makeup, she was a beautiful girl. Her tall lithe body looked good in the faded jeans. I was almost sorry that I wouldn't be able to keep our Friday date.

"I just learned something interesting," I said. She looked in my direction but more out of courtesy than curiosity. "Seems the old man who had the ring was actually Vicki Johnson's father. How's that for coincidence?" Gail bristled at the mention of the girl's name. Perhaps it was my imagination, but it seemed like she was more touchy than normal whenever I mentioned the incident.

"Well, that certainly explains a lot of things, doesn't it?"

"Yes and no," I replied. "It sure explains the relationship but the question of what happened to the rest of the treasure is still unsolved. And it also raises the question of whether Vicki Johnson may still be alive. Have you seen anybody around her apartment?"

"No, not at all," Gail said matter-of-factly. I was beginning to get the impression that she knew the missing girl better than she had first indicated. While in the kitchen, I noticed that the sink was full of dirty dishes, more than one person could have used unless she hadn't run any through the dishwasher in about three days. As she talked sitting on the sofa, the large ashtray on the coffee table happened to catch my eye. It was fairly full of cigarette butts with lipstick on the filters. There was also burned tobacco in several neat little piles.

"Do you have a roommate?" Gail caught me looking at the ashtray and read my thoughts.

"Oh no, I had some friends over last night and haven't gotten around to cleaning up."

Strange, I thought to myself. She supposedly has the flu but throws a party?

"Well I'm sure you have to get back and write your stories," Gail said, standing up and walking toward the door – my cue to go.

"Yes. Thank you for the use of your phone. And we'll have to make that date for another time."

"Right, I'll look forward to hearing from you," she said as I made my way out onto the open, second floor corridor.

"One more thing, Gail," I said, turning around. "I understand that the Johnson girl was on vacation the week before the incident at the museum. Did you see her around? At the pool or in the recreation room?"

"No," Gail said emphatically. "Like I said, I didn't know her except to see her by the pool once or twice. If I did see her, I don't remember. We just didn't travel in the same crowds."

"I remember you telling me. Hope you get to feeling better."

The editors of the various departments were gathered in the conference room for their daily afternoon budget meeting to determine what stories they had for tomorrow's paper when I got back to the newsroom. I held up ten fingers through the open doorway, indicating to Max that I would have a ten inch story for the metro section. After checking the mailbox, I walked back to my desk near the photo department. Tracy was hunched over the desk with the phone in her ear. With her big hornrimmed glasses on the end of her nose, she was madly scribbling on a legal pad. I went through my mail until she had finished her call.

"Have any luck?" she asked, rubbing the pain in her neck. It's an affliction that attacks newsmen who spend most of their time wrapped around an uncomfortable telephone receiver.

"Not bad," I replied. "How about you?"

"For starters, I called the office of Bridge Inspections in Tallahassee and found out that Mr. Eisenberg was working the night of the robbery."

"Working?" I asked. "Why should they be inspecting bridges on a Saturday night?"

"He wasn't. At least not that they're aware of. You see, each of the inspectors take turns being on call each weekend in case there's an emergency like a boat ramming the pilings and they get called in to check for damage."

"Was there any record of him working that night?"

"None. But then he lives alone and told police that he was home that night so there's

194

no way of checking out his story," Tracy said, laying her glasses on top of her notes.

"Does he live in Tallahassee?"

"No, here in Jacksonville. The director said that his office is responsible for all bridges in the northwest quadrant of the state. And since most of the bridges are in or around Jacksonville, he said most of his inspectors live over here."

"Do you have an address?"

"Not yet. But I understand he rents an apartment somewhere near the beach."

"Okay. What else you got?" The clock above the metro desk showed 6:20 P.M. – about an hour before first edition deadline.

"Lieutenant Marler got an answer back from Washington on that man burned in the hotel fire yesterday. Seems his name was Walters instead of Smith. He evidently spent several years in the Merchant Marine. Marler said he had a small arrest record but just minor stuff like petty larceny."

"He was also Vicki Johnson's father," I said, trying to sound as nonchalant as I could.

"Really?" Tracy said. "Who told you?"

"The foreman over at the warehouse. Said he's been sitting on it because he is afraid he'll lose his job once the word is out. However, I still think that Hall fellow is awfully squirrely and somehow is mixed up in this thing."

"Did you talk to him?"

"Yes, but didn't learn much. Let me sit down there and have a shot at that typewriter and then we'll go grab some dinner."

After thirty-five minutes of sweating over my story, I dropped the copy off at the metro desk and Tracy and I headed for the parking lot.

"Where to tonight?" she asked.

"Great little seafood restaurant out toward the beach on the river. It's a nice place – where the fishing boats tie up. You'll love it."

The road to the restaurant is a twisting ribbon of blacktop that parallels the river north of town. It was dark out and the headlights of the Mustang shone into the oak trees and reflected on the thick clumps of Spanish Moss hanging from the limbs at every turn. Rounding a sharp turn about ten minutes from the restaurant, we could easily make out the flashing blue lights of police cars a mile ahead of us. As we got closer, I could see a small car rolled over on its side. One patrolman was standing in the middle of the road with a flashlight directing traffic.

"Hi, officer. What have we got here?"

"Hello, Brad," he said through the open window of the car. "A single fatality. Looks like he lost control in that dirt over there."

"Sorry, Tracy, but I better get a few

details while we're here," I said, pulling the convertible onto the dirt shoulder. "Why don't you stay in the car? I won't be but a second."

Officers had uprighted the crumpled Volkswagen by the time I walked across the street. The evidence technician had his camera out and was snapping pictures of the dead man behind the wheel. Standing nearby was a traffic homicide investigator whom I recognized interviewing a witness that saw the man lose control of the car. She was telling the investigator how it happened and he was making notes in a little pad. One of the evidence people said something to one of the officers who then went up and grabbed the victim by the hair. Holding the head toward the driver's side of the car, the other policeman began snapping pictures of the grisly scene that would eventually end up in the accident file.

After the traffic homicide investigator was through talking to the witness, I interviewed him and got the notes I needed. As I finished, two attendants from the medical examiner's office arrived to take the body to the morgue.

"Hey, Nick. What you know?" I yelled to one of the attendants. He gave a nod and began helping pull the dead man's body out of the car. After they had him into a body bag and secured in the back of the station wagon, I asked the attendant if they had identified the drowning victim from earlier in the day.

"Hey, man, I don't know nothing about it."

"What do you mean, you don't know anything about it. You were there this morning, remember? I saw you there. What's the big deal, anyway? Just a drowning victim, right?"

"I mean I don't know whether they have identified the body yet. I just pick 'em up. The Doc does the rest."

"Who are you kidding?" I asked. "We're not talking about some big hospital. That place is so small nothing goes on down there that you don't know about. I just want to run a digest item in the roundup so I don't get scooped. That isn't too much to ask, is it?"

"Give me a break, will 'ya? Can't you see I got my hands full? You got any questions, call the Doc. He'll tell you what you want to know."

"Yeah, thanks," I said over my shoulder as I walked back toward the car. Once behind the wheel, I stared out the window for a second as I decided what to do.

"Pretty bad?" Tracy asked, referring to the accident.

"Yeah," I said, "but I think we better

198

go down to the medical examiner's office. Something doesn't smell right and I want to know what it is."

"Can't it wait?" she pleaded. "I'm starved."

"It'll only take a second. They've identified that woman and I want to know what the big secret is about."

11

Dr. Lin, Marler and two strangers in dark blue suits were talking when Tracy and I walked through the windowed double doors of the morgue's examining room. The grim outline of a body on a high metal table could be seen beneath a white sheet on one side of the yellow-tiled room. Gone from view was the body of Ike Smith as well as the two other men killed in the fire at the Ashton Hotel the day before. As we walked in, the four men all had the same identical look on their faces – sheer panic.

"Norris, what the hell are you doing here?"

"Just thought we'd drop by and see what was going on, Lieutenant. What is going on, by the way?"

Dr. Lin placed his glasses on top of his forehead and rubbed his eyes with his index finger and thumb as he talked. "I was just telling the policemen here . . ."

"That's enough, Doc. You don't have to tell them anything right now," Marler interrupted.

I opened my notebook and began making notes on everything said. It's a little trick I use whenever a source decides he doesn't want to talk about a subject. Just stand there and stare long enough, jotting notes, and he comes around every time. I've only printed such a one-sided interview a couple of times, but the idea works so well, I'm rarely ever forced to follow through.

"C'mon, Lieutenant, we've been walking the ledge too long on this thing to start playing games, don't you think?"

"Look, Norris, just back off a little bit and give us time to put this thing together, okay? You'll get the story. Just give us a little breathing room."

"Fine. I'll give you all the room you need. But for starters, how about leveling with me? It concerns the body on that examining table over there doesn't it? The woman discovered in the borrow pit this morning?"

Marler did not speak but Dr. Lin's face indicated that I was on the right track. The two men in blue suits were standing there glaring with their arms crossed but obviously perplexed as to what action they should take.

"I'm telling you, Norris, if you don't get out of here, I'm gonna have you thrown in jail." I continued writing in my notebook and only returned his stare. After what seemed like several minutes, the homicide detective finally shrugged his shoulders and glanced at Lin.

"All right. As long as you're here. But you print one word of this before I give the okay and I'll get the State Attorney to sue that damn paper of yours, you got that?"

"Fine," I replied. "Message noted. Now fill me in. The woman you found — Vicki Johnson, right?" I could almost hear Tracy's mouth fall open behind me.

"Hey, you know so much, how come you're snooping around here?" Marler asked.

"I get paid to snoop, remember? Now, what did you find?"

Dr. Lin slipped the black hornrimmed glasses on top of his head back onto the bridge of his nose and began thumbing through a file he had been holding at his side. "The body was badly decomposed as you saw this morning. However, we have been able to determine that the victim did not die from

201

drowning. There was no significant traces of water found in the lungs."

"Interesting," I replied. "So if she didn't drown, how did she die?"

"If you would like to step over here, I'd be glad to show you," Lin said, gesturing toward the body with the sheet draped over it. I felt Tracy's cold grip on my arm.

"Thanks, Doc, but I don't think that will be necessary."

"Oh yes, I see," he said, turning back toward the center of the room. "In any event, it seems she died of strangulation. The larynx and portions of the esophagus were crushed. And there were several bruises in the vicinity of the collarbone."

"From what? A hammer or piece of pipe, maybe?"

"We can't be sure at this point," he continued, looking at me over the tops of his bi-focals. "But it doesn't look as if any sort of blunt instrument was used. The contusions were too general. No, I believe the victim died at the hands of a person with a very strong grip."

"How about other bruises? Any broken bones or something that might have been caused by a fall from a great height?"

"You mean like a bridge? Nothing we've been able to find yet indicates such a thing.

There were some lacerations on her shins and calves which may have been caused by rope or wire which in turn was tied to weights in an attempt to hold the body at the bottom of the lake. However, we haven't got the results of all the tests yet. Won't have the final report until morning."

"Well, at least now we know she wasn't in this thing alone," I said turning in Marler's direction. "And I doubt if her father had anything to do with her death."

"Think maybe she was involved with somebody from Mediterranean Maritime?" asked Tracy.

"Perhaps," I replied. "The foreman at the warehouse – I think his name was Callahan – he certainly had the strength to do something like that," I added, nodding toward the girl's remains.

"The big question is where do we go from here?" Marler continued, taking a cigarette from his coat pocket.

"The bridge."

"Bridge?" he repeated, exhaling a puff of smoke into the center of the room. "What about the bridge?"

"That's where we go from here," I said. "Under it, over it, on it – there must be something we overlooked that will give us a clue as to how they pulled this thing off."

Early Friday morning, I was waiting in Marler's office when he came back from the morning staff meeting. I wanted him to join me in my investigation of the bridge.

"I told you last night, Norris. You're not going to find anything on that bridge. And I'm not about to hold up traffic while you go snooping around. That's the only reason you want me along anyway – figure with me there, the bridge people won't be as likely to throw you off."

"Let's face it, Lieutenant. It's a stab in the dark but the only stab you have going at the moment, right? I mean, what other leads you working on? Maybe one or two, but the chances of them turning into anything are next to none. C'mon, what do you have to lose? We'll just take a quick drive over the span and won't cause any big deals, promise."

Fortunately, late-morning traffic was light by the time we arrived. Marler parked his car in the eastbound lane closest to the railing. While I tried to determine the exact point from which the woman had jumped, the detective stayed behind, partly to protect the car, although I don't know what he would have done had someone slammed into the rear.

"Here, Lieutanant," I yelled. "This is the

spot where the girl went over the side."

"I'm impressed," said Marler. "Now, is there anything else you'd like to show me before I go back to the office?"

"One more minute," I pleaded. The portion of the center span which served as the roadway was actually steel grating rather than asphalt – a design popular in bridges for two reasons, I later learned. First of all, it is lighter than concrete at a key location where weight is critical. Secondly, the perforated steel allows for maximum drainoff of rain and snow, thereby reducing the chance of accidents.

Gazing through the small holes at the green water far below, I suddenly noticed some sort of catwalk fifteen feet below the level of the span upon which I was standing.

"What's that?" I asked.

"What's what?"

"Down there. Looks like some sort of gangplank."

"Oh that. It's a catwalk they use for mainte-nance and stuff. My men have already been down there and didn't find a thing."

"How do you get down?"

"This piece of grating lifts up ... but what do you want to go down there for? I already told you, my men checked it out and found nothing."

"It's like the journalism business, Lieutenant. First you check your facts and then you check them again. I don't think it will hurt to look once more, do you?"

"Well, you better hurry or you're gonna spend more time down there than you planned."

The small metal ladder descended twelve feet to the narrow walkway below. The small metal structure was attached to the broad concrete girders. Running perpendicular to the center span, the walkway extended almost the full width of the bridge. Like the span above, it was painted gun-metal gray. There was barely room to turn around. I spent a minute or two crawling to the southern end of the catwalk. Above me was the spot on the span where I had been standing only a few minutes before. It was a breathtaking view – the only thing between me and the cold green water below was one hundred fifty feet. I became so enamored of the view of the city from my vantage point, I almost missed noticing the scratches on the railing.

"Lieutenant," I yelled. "Can you hear me?"

"Yeah, what d'ya want?" came the reply through the grating above.

"Come down here a minute. I want to show you something."

"No way. I'm not climbing down on that rickety ol' thing. You can show me from here."

"It's perfectly safe," I yelled back. "Besides, you're going to want to see this."

After five minutes, Marler made his way out to the end of the catwalk, gripping the safety rails on both sides of the narrow walkway with skinny white knuckles. "Norris, for your sake, this better be worth it."

"It is – look at this," I said, pointing to the marks on the railing.

"Scratch marks," he said, his fear of heights suddenly being replaced with a slow-burning anger in the pit of his stomach. "You made me go through this trapeze act for scratch marks? Why, you dumb son-of . . ."

"Lieutenant, if you'll shut up long enough for me to explain, I'll show you the significance of the marks. Look closely and you can see no rust has built up in these grooves yet. These scratches are fairly fresh – at least, within the last month or so."

Marler leaned forward as far as he dared and studied the gashes made through the several coats of gray paint to the raw steel beneath.

"Two weeks ago," I continued, "when the Johnson woman jumped off the bridge, I noticed the same marks on the railing above us. It was the exact spot from which she jumped, according to the cop who was chasing her. At the time, I figured they were probably made by a belt buckle."

"You think maybe she hit this railing on the way down?" Marler asked.

"In a manner of speaking," I replied. "Except this was as far as she went. The catwalk is almost directly beneath the spot where she jumped. I think her leap off the bridge wasn't a back-against-the-wall suicidal tendency. I think she purposely planned to jump off this bridge. The perfect getaway."

"Yeah, it makes sense. She had a rope tied to the railing here and swung underneath the bridge and out of sight."

"Makes you feel kind of dumb, doesn't it, Lieutenant? We're all up there looking for her and she was lying right here watching us the whole time."

"I suppose you're going to have to run back and print all of this, aren't you?"

"Now, honestly, wouldn't you?"

Instead of answering, Marler elected to change the subject. "Supposing she did lower herself onto this platform that night. How do you figure she got away?"

"Simple," I continued. "Either crawled out through the hole in the grating after everybody had gone or possibly lowered herself down to the water below and was picked up by a waiting boat."

"Seems like somebody would have seen her climbing out of that hole," Marler pondered. "But then, that girl in the morgue didn't look like she was in any kind of shape to climb down one hundred fifty feet of rope."

"I know it doesn't seem practical. But since the whole thing was planned, who knows what kind of mechanical contraptions she could have stored down here prior to that night."

"I still don't see how a woman could have climbed around this bridge through traffic and all, without being spotted. But climbing down to the water would explain how the money bag ended up on the river bank over there," he said, pointing to the spot where the bag containing the coin was found. "Seems kind of stupid to leave the evidence behind. But whoever was in this with her must have transferred the treasure to something else and pitched the bag."

"Right. And since they probably made their getaway in the dark, they might have thrown it farther than they thought, expecting it to sink in the water instead of ending up on the river bank."

Marler became a little more relaxed dangling above the water as he sat down on the metal catwalk with his back to the railing. "But if that's the case – if she lowered herself down there," he said, looking between the open spaces in the bottom of the walkway, "how did she get rid of the rope? I mean, our men would have found it the next day. At least a glove or something."

"I know. She sure left this place clean – almost as if she were in no hurry. I don't know how she did it. But at least we have a little more to go on."

"For now, let's get off this thing before it collapses." Carefully retracing his steps along the catwalk, Marler crawled through the opening in the grating. I followed him up.

Back at the police station, I found Tracy in the tiny cubicle which serves as a press room, reading an old copy of *"Editor and Publisher."* The only furniture in the room consists of a scratched up old wooden table and two metal chairs with the padding half gone. As for modern mechanical devices of the trade, there is a teletype which connects with a corresponding model in the newsroom across town and a battered up old Royal typewriter with a ribbon so worn it leaves an imprint barely readable.

I pulled one of the uncomfortable chairs up to the teletype and began typing the story I had so far into the machine. It was a convenient system since I could file my stories right from the police station and didn't have to drive across town.

"Run down anything new this morning?" I asked as I punched the red plastic keys.

"Not really," Tracy said. "By the way, Dr. Lin called and wanted to talk to you. He wouldn't tell me what it was about. Seemed kind of secretive about the whole thing."

"Okay. I'll give him a call as soon as I type in the rest of these notes."

"Did you find anything at the bridge?"

"Yes, figured out how she did it – pulled it off, I mean."

"Really," Tracy said, looking up from the magazine. "How's that?"

"There's a catwalk that runs beneath the bridge. And there are marks in the paint both on the railing where she actually jumped and on the catwalk below. She apparently swung underneath on some sort of rope contraption."

"The whole thing is strange, isn't it? Vicki Johnson is found floating in a lake fifteen miles from the river and her father is burned to death in a hotel fire a week later. There are still so many questions unanswered," she said. Tracy was an incredibly beautiful woman with long silky legs beneath her tan-colored skirt. The brown sandals with leather heels she was wearing blended perfectly with the dark tan which even extended to her feet and ankles. I found it hard to concentrate on the teletype as she sat there looking so gorgeous, cleaning her plastic glasses with a borrowed handkerchief.

After transmitting the remainder of my notes over the lumbersome old machine, I called the medical examiner's office.

"Hi, Doc! Brad Norris. What's up?"

"Have you talked with Lieutenant Marler yet?"

"Not since we got back from the bridge. Why?" I asked.

"I'd better not say," Lin said at the other end of the line. I could tell by the tone of his voice that he had made some sort of major discovery and was wrestling with his conscience as to whether he should let me in on the secret.

"Why don't you check with Lieutenant Marler. But don't let him know I put you up to it."

"Aw, come on, Doc. I'm all the way at the other end of the building and he's out of the office right now," I said, hoping the doctor would buy my bluff. "Why don't you tell me and I'll pretend I got the word from one of his detectives. I'll keep you out of it like I always do, promise."

There was a moment or two before Lin's voice interrupted the silence on the other end of the line. "The woman . . ."

"Vicki Johnson?" I asked.

"Yes," he replied. "I can't be sure, mind you. But our tests indicate she was murdered three to four days before she supposedly jumped off the bridge."

"Are you sure?" I blurted into the receiver.

"No, like I just told you, there's no way of being positive in something like this. Especially when the body has undergone extensive decomposition like Miss Johnson's. Off the record though, I'd say we're about eighty percent sure that she wasn't around to jump off of any bridge that night."

"Thanks for the information," I said, hanging up the pressroom phone.

"What about Vicky Johnson?" Tracy asked.

"According to Lin, she was dead before the incident on the bridge took place. Somebody obviously went to a lot of trouble to make it look like she pulled this whole thing off."

"Now where do we go?"

The news from Dr. Lin triggered something in my mind – reminded me of something I had intended to do at the Sand Flea Apartments the day before but had forgotten about. Looking up the number in the phone book, I called the manager of the complex and talked to her for several minutes.

"What was that all about?" Tracy asked as I hung up the receiver.

"Vicki Johnson lived at a singles complex on the eastside. While I was over there yesterday, I stopped by and talked to a girl named Gail Tomlinson who also lives there. Ironically, she manages the museum that the jewels were stolen from. She said she didn't know Vicki which I thought was strange for a singles complex. I mean, those places are known for their mingling, right? So I called the manager to check out her story."

"And?"

"According to her, Gail Tomlinson and our murdered victim were more than nodding acquaintances. She doesn't know how close they really were, but did say she saw Vicki come out of Gail's apartment maybe a half dozen times in the last couple of months. Which is a lot closer than Gail led me to believe."

"So you think she may be involved?"

"At least a good suspect."

"You going to tell the lieutenant?"

"No. You are," I replied. "I want you to go tell him what we know so far. Considering Gail's position, she must be bonded. See if

214

Marler can get some kind of make on her. I'll be back in about half an hour."

"Where are you going?"

"I thought after Marler and I got back this morning that we should have stopped by the bridge toll office to see if anybody on duty that night saw anything."

"But the bridge tolls are on the east side of the bridge and the girl – I mean, whoever jumped off the bridge – drove on the bridge from the west side," Tracy said as we walked into the main hallway of the police building.

"I know that. But you never can tell – somebody might have been on a break and been walking along the bank when all the activity took place. And even if Vicki Johnson wasn't involved, we know that somebody was on that catwalk recently."

After introducing myself to the manager of the Andover Bridge toll booth office, I waited in a small reception room inside the side door. According to him, there were only two people on duty who were also working the night of the incident. I leafed through an old *Time* magazine while waiting for the two employees to come off duty.

After waiting forty-five minutes, two women – one in her mid twenties and the other in her late forties – walked through the side door that faces the employee parking lot and sat on the leather sofa across from me. The younger woman didn't talk much and seemed anxious to leave. However, the older of the two seemed cooperative, although she admitted not remembering much of the Saturday night two weeks before.

"I wish I could help you, but I really didn't see anything unusual. It was a pretty normal night, really." As she talked, the woman fingered a key ring with a leather fob attached. The letter B was burned into the brown shiny leather.

"How about the other people that worked that night? Do you remember anybody mentioning anything that was out of the ordinary?"

"No, I don't. About the only thing different was the traffic. After the woman jumped up there, cars in the opposite lane slowed down to look as they drove past. And that caused a bit of a bottleneck down here at the toll booths."

"But you didn't see anybody jump off the bridge or anything out of the ordinary?"

"You really can't see much from down here, anyway, Mr. Norris," she replied. "'Specially in the dark. We could see the policeman's lights and stuff like that. But that was about it. Just the police, rescue, and the bridge people, stuff like that. Most of us were so busy with

216

the traffic backed up, we didn't have time to do much looking." I noticed out of the corner of my eye that the young woman wouldn't be able to contain herself much longer.

"Well, thanks for taking the time to talk with me," I said, standing up and taking a business card out of my shirt pocket. "Would you talk to the other people who worked that night and see if they remember anything? I would appreciate a call if you turn up anything."

As I turned to walk out the door to the parking lot, something the woman had said turned over in my mind. "Excuse me, but you mentioned bridge people. What bridge people?"

"You know, bridge people," she replied. "I didn't see anybody specifically, mind you. But one of their trucks went through my gate about two or three hours after it happened, the girl jumping I mean."

"You're talking about one of those orange and yellow pickup trucks the bridge inspection people drive?"

"Yeah, that's the type. Came through my toll gate after the woman's car was towed off and things returned to normal. Skinny little kid was driving. Had a hard hat pulled down over his face. I asked him if he'd been called to come out and inspect the bridge on

217

account of all the activity and he said 'yep'. That's all he said – a real talkative type, you know?"

"Know what you mean," I answered. "That's pretty unusual for them to work such weird hours, isn't it?"

"Sure, unless they're blasting or painting or something. But those inspection guys got it real cushy – regular banker's hours, you know. But they always have one of 'em on call in case a ship rams the pilings or something bad happens. There's a number on the bulletin board that we're supposed to call in case we need them."

"Would you call?"

"Nope. That would be up to the watch supervisor on duty."

"Do you know whether he called that night?"

"No, I don't."

"Well, thanks again for your time."

"You're welcome," she replied. "Is my name gonna be in the paper tomorrow?"

"Let's hope so," I replied. It's easier than trying to explain that I'm just fishing for information.

Before leaving, I checked with the manager again to see if the watch supervisor on duty the night of the incident had called the emergency number requesting a bridge inspector. The records indicated that no such call had been made.

Back at the police station, Tracy was sitting in the homicide section outside Marler's office when I walked in. I was followed into the room by a detective in a short-sleeved yellow shirt carrying a police revolver in a detachable leather holster.

"Okay, which one of you clowns left your gun in the bathroom," he announced to the half-dozen policemen sitting at their desks in various positions. Everyone checked under his left armpit to make sure he wasn't guilty.

"Not here," yelled one plainclothes officer from the back of the room. "Try robbery. Those guys are losing something all the time."

"Yeah, and not just their guns," said another, evoking a chuckle from all in the room.

As the detective disappeared down the hallway in the direction of the robbery section, Marler came out of his office with a cup of coffee in his hand.

"Got anything back on the Tomlinson girl yet?" I asked.

"Not yet. What makes you think she's involved?"

"To begin with, she lied about knowing Vicki Johnson. Said they barely knew each other, but the manager of the apartment says

219

different. Also, I noticed when I was in her apartment the other day she had company for breakfast that morning because there were dishes in the sink for at least two."

"Having somebody spend the evening isn't exactly a felony, you know," Marler said, leaning against the door frame of his office.

"No, but I also noticed burnt tobacco in an ashtray in the living room. Burnt tobacco with no paper around it. The type a person would smoke in a pipe."

"Quite a detective we have here. So what does it all mean, Mr. Holmes?"

"Just a hunch," I replied. "But Stuart Eisenberg smokes a pipe."

"And you think he's tied up in this thing too?"

"Yes I do. As a matter of fact, I'll bet he's at her apartment right now. Care to go over for a little chat?"

"Not unless you have a little more to go on," Marler said.

"I do, but let's not waste any further time here. I'm afraid the two of them may try to split if they get suspicious. If you have somebody over that way, I think it would be a good idea to have both their apartments staked out."

It took several rings of the doorbell before the front door opened to reveal part of Gail

Tomlinson's face behind the chain, which was still locked.

"Miss Tomlinson, I'm Lieutenant Marler, do you remember? We'd like to talk to you for a moment."

Gail stared at us with large unblinking eyes. She seemed as much at a loss for words as she had the day before. "I'm afraid I can't at the moment. You see, I . . ."

"Won't take a second, Miss," Marler said with a little more determination. "If you'll please unlock the door?"

With unblinking eyes, Gail unlatched the chain and opened the door, allowing us to enter. "What's this all about?" she asked in a broken voice.

"I understand you barely knew Vicki Johnson, is that correct?" Marler continued.

"We spoke a few times at the pool," Gail said, her questioning eyes turning toward me for some sort of explanation and then back to the lieutenant. "But not real well."

"Come now, Miss Tomlinson, we've done a little checking on you. We know, for example, that you attended college in St. Petersburg – the same college, in fact, where Vicki Johnson went to school for a year and a half before dropping out."

"Oh really?" The pretty lady was beginning to crack under the interrogation. "Then

221

you're probably aware that it is a large campus and the possibility for two people to go to school there and not know each other is rather large."

"Yes, possible," Marler said with a faint smile. "But during the summer between your junior and senior year of college, didn't you work on a Key West boat helping a certain company look for Spanish treasure? A company called Off Shore Divers?" I was a little shocked at that point. Marler had more background on her than I had realized and had been holding back.

"Y-yes, that's all true, but it still doesn't prove anything."

"Gail," I said, "Vicki Johnson was dead before the museum was robbed. You worked for Furman during the excavation of the treasure. And you were also handling the treasure at the museum. No signs of forced entry, remember?"

"But I was at a party in the clubhouse downstairs when the museum was robbed. You can check and see for yourself."

"You didn't rob the treasure. Stuart Eisenberg did. He was on duty that night, but the girl at the toll booth said a skinny kid wearing a hard hat drove through her booth in the truck. That skinny kid was you, right? Going to pick up Eisenberg, who was hiding on the catwalk beneath the center span?"

At that point, Gail sank to the living room couch and broke into uncontrolled sobs. "I didn't want to kill her. I didn't want her dead."

"Where can we find Eisenberg?" Marler asked as he walked toward the phone in the kitchen.

"I don't know," she said between tears. "Maybe his apartment at the beach."

Stuart Eisenberg, it turned out, lived in a spacious garden apartment in Atlantic Beach. It was one of six units located in the complex four blocks from the beach.

Marler had radioed from Gail's apartment, so several detectives had the complex under surveillance by the time we arrived. Marler allowed me to ride with him provided I stay out of his way. By that, he meant out of sight and earshot.

About two blocks from the complex, Marler pulled up beside a white Chevrolet and rolled down his window.

"What have we got, Lou?" he asked the man behind the wheel of the white car.

"Apartment's empty, Lieutenant. According to the woman who keeps an eye on the place, he hasn't been around all morning. Most of the people who live in the complex work so the area is pretty vacant."

"Okay, let's sit tight for a minute and see what turns up." Marler picked up the microphone to his two-way radio and keyed the Zone Four dispatcher. "This is Lieutenant Marler and I want an APB put out on Stuart Eisenberg," he said. "He's an employee of the Department of Bridges and Highways and drives one of those orange and yellow pickup trucks. I want you to call the department and get the license plate number of his truck and put it out. But I want it kept code 'S' with no one near him."

In about five minutes, we heard the dispatcher give an all-points bulletin over the radio for Eisenberg's truck.

Marler had parked his car on a side street next to some bushes so we were well-concealed. I watched a group of kids carrying towels and beach toys as they walked down the street in front of us. The hot sun shining through the windshield made me sleepy. The quiet was only occasionally interrupted by the sound of the police radio which Marler had turned down very low.

"What do you think, Lieutenant? Possible Eisenberg may have been tipped off?"

"Possible. But I don't see how. We weren't even on to him until a couple of hours ago. And he would have taken the Tomlinson girl with him if he was going to leave."

"Maybe. And maybe he decided to split and leave her behind."

"What? And spill her guts to us once she realized what he'd done? I rather doubt it."

"You're right. He must still be in the area. But where?"

"Don't move an inch but I'll tell you where," Marler said as he stared into the rear view mirror. "He's going to pass us in a second." No sooner had the lieutenant spoken than the familiar yellow and orange pickup truck drove past us. When the truck had passed through the intersection in front of us, Marler got on the radio and informed all of the other detectives that their suspect was about to enter their trap.

"Got him, chief," said a voice on the radio. "He's in front of the complex now."

Marler started the engine and pulled the Dodge out into the street.

"Hey, he's not stopping!" the voice continued. "I don't know whether he saw us or not but he's going to run."

"Keep on his tail," Marler said into the microphone. "But don't rush him yet. Give him plenty of room."

The pickup truck turned south on A1A and then west on Atlantic Boulevard as it headed toward Jacksonville. Marler passed the other detectives until he was one hundred yards behind Eisenberg. Traffic on the highway was light.

"Do you think he knows we're behind him, Lieutenant?"

"I don't know. He's not really pushing it. I don't know what he's doing."

Marler called for a roadblock ahead and the pickup truck accelerated until it was doing eighty miles per hour. Marler turned on his lights and siren. But Eisenberg paid no attention.

"The bridge," I said. "Maybe he plans to do something at the bridge."

"What can he do? We're already wise to him. And besides, he'll have to run that roadblock first."

The chase continued for fifteen miles and through several red lights. Fortunately, patrol cars had been set up ahead to stop him before he got to downtown Jacksonville. The Andover Bridge was now coming into view. Before long we could make out the patrol cars ahead, blocking the four-lane highway with their blue lights flashing.

"Think he'll stop?" I asked.

"He doesn't have much choice. Unless, of course, he kills himself trying to drive through there."

And that is exactly what it looked like Eisenberg was going to do. He drove straight toward the patrol cars at top speed before locking the brakes and going into a side-spin. The patrolmen who had been standing behind their cars began to run for cover. Fifteen feet from the cars, Eisenberg regained control of the truck and aimed it toward a grassy embankment by the side of the road. He was almost to the top of the rise and near escaping when one of the sharpshooters with the police department's S.W.A.T. team drew a bead on the truck and shot out the right rear tire. Eisenberg jumped from the cab and began running up the hill but was soon captured by a couple of cops who had been waiting at the top of the embankment.

"Morgan, I want you to take a couple of guys and go back and check out his apartment. See if you can find any sign of the treasure," Marler said as they handcuffed Eisenberg and put him into the back seat of a nearby patrol car. "I'll call you if he tells us anything."

Per my instructions, Tracy had called the paper for a photographer and Wink was standing by near the parking lot entrance of the police station with camera in hand when we arrived.

"Nice going," he said. "Solved the case, huh?"

"Part of it, at least," I replied.

12

After writing up the story for Saturday morning's edition, Tracy and I celebrated with a big dinner and a bottle of wine. Then we went back to Marler's office to see what other details had been uncovered in the case.

"What'd you book him on, Lieutenant?"

"A host of crimes including robbery and murder one for starters."

"Then he did kill Vicki Johnson?"

"No doubt about it. Seems the three of 'em were actually in this thing together. The two girls knew each other from school and then became reacquainted when they moved to Jacksonville about a year and a half ago. Eisenberg dated the Tomlinson girl and when it became evident the treasure would be on display here, they began planning the robbery."

"So Furman knew all along that Gail was familiar with the treasure but still played like he didn't know her," Tracy said.

"That's right," Marler continued, "but we don't think he's really mixed up in this thing. More likely, he figured it was coincidence and knew it would put extra pressure on Gail if we found out about her connection."

"So why did they kill her?" I asked, jotting a few notes in my legal pad.

"Simple. Vicki Johnson got cold feet about four days before the scheduled heist. When it became apparent that she might come to us, Eisenberg killed her, drove to the borrow pit and dumped her body in the middle of the lake after weighting it down with concrete blocks."

"And after she was dead, he decided that dressing up like her and using her car in the fake leap off the bridge would be the perfect cover-up as to her disappearance, right?"

"Right. But what turned you on to Eisenberg in the first place?" Marler asked.

"He seemed like the perfect suspect although I wasn't positive until the girl from the toll booth confirmed that he was on the bridge that night. Eisenberg knew more about that bridge than anybody – had probably been on that catwalk a million times. Unlike both of the women, he also had the muscles to swing under the bridge and hide on the walkway until the coast was clear."

"But who picked him up?" asked Tracy.

"Gail Tomlinson did but not in a boat as we first thought," I continued. "Dressed in work clothes and a hard hat pulled down over her face, she drove the orange and yellow inspection truck onto the bridge after we had all gone. Then she parked far enough over the grating cover so that Eisenberg could slip into the back of the truck unnoticed. And since the truck spends so much time around the bridge, no one questioned the vehicle stopped in the center of the bridge."

"But then how did the money bag end up at the foot of the bridge? And how did Vicki Johnson's father come into possession of the rings?" Tracy was asking the questions as fast as Marler could answer them.

"According to Gail Tomlinson, that was a freak chain of events. Evidently, she had picked up Eisenberg and they were both driving off the bridge when they noticed that the police had set up a roadblock at the foot of the bridge and were spot-checking cars as they passed through. Eisenberg knew that the area beneath the bridge was grassy and unpopulated so he threw the bag containing the jewels over the side before they got to the police blockade. Then after passing through, they doubled back and picked up the bag."

"Yeah, but that still doesn't explain how Ike Smith got mixed up in this thing," I asked.

"We're not really sure what happened at that point. The only thing we can figure is that since Ike slept around there, he had probably been watching all the activity above and found the bag that Eisenberg threw over the side. When he saw the headlights of the inspection truck coming toward him a few minutes later, he must have realized they were looking for the treasure. Had he taken all the jewels, he figured they wouldn't have stopped looking until they had found the gems and him, too. Instead, he took just a handful and left the rest for the unsuspecting duo."

"Kind of dumb for Eisenberg to leave the bank bag down there as evidence, wasn't it?"

"He didn't," Marler said, lighting up a cigarette. "He didn't even use that bag until later. It wasn't until he saw your article in the paper about Smith's body being found with the ring on his finger that he decided to go back and plant that dummy bag with the doubloon inside it. Vicki had mentioned that her old man hung around the area. Eisenberg couldn't have planned the whole thing better."

"You mean to tell me that the father and daughter were both involved in this thing by accident and didn't know about each other?" Tracy asked.

"As far as we're concerned, yes," Marler said as he slipped the butane lighter back into the pocket of his doubleknit pants.

"Well, anyway you look at it, this is one of the most intriguing stories we've ever had in Jacksonville for some time," I said, closing the cover of my legal pad.

"And I hope the last," Marler added.

"How about the treasure?" Tracy asked, getting up from her chair.

"Most of it was recovered in Eisenberg's apartment," he said, grabbing his sports coat off the rack near the front door of the homicide office. As we were all walking out the door, the phone on the secretary's desk rang and Marler answered it.

"That was your boss, Norris," he said as he hung up the receiver. "Seems there's a story breaking over in Lake City that he wants you to drive over and investigate."

"Hell, it's almost ten o'clock now and Lake City is a good hour's drive from here. How am I supposed to get a story in time?"

"That's your problem," Marler said with a smile. "I'm just delighted that it's out of my territory for a change. At least, you'll be out of my hair for a while."

"Cute," I said as Tracy and I walked through the parking lot and climbed into the Mustang. "Just wait till you see what kind of treatment I give you in the paper tomorrow."

"Can't be any worse than what you've already written about me," he answered.

"You know me, Lieutenant. I always strive to present our readers with the truth."

With a squeal of tires, Marler's green Dodge disappeared into the darkness of night.

"No sense of humor," I mockingly added. "Pretty good cop but holds no promise as a reporter."

"Thank God for small favors," Tracy said. "With you around, who needs competition."

Traffic on the expressway leading to Lake City was light for a Friday night.

alt- 11-30-90